SURVIVING THE STORM

SHANE KROETSCH

Surviving the Storm

Copyright © Shane Kroetsch

All rights reserved

First edition October 2020

No part of this book may be reproduced in any manner whatsoever without the prior written permission of the author, except in the case of brief quotations in a book review.

This story is a work of fiction. Names, characters, places, and incidents are either the product of the author's imagination or are used fictitiously. Any resemblance to actual persons, living or undead, or actual events, is coincidental.

Pencil on Paper
Airdrie, Alberta
Canada
www.pencilonpaper.ca

ISBN 978-1-9994820-6-0 (paperback)

ISBN 978-1-9994820-7-7 (ebook)

Cover design by Francois Vaillancourt

CONTENT WARNING

This story contains scenes of graphic violence and death, gore, gun violence, and suicide.

For those who refuse to give up.

ONE

Jacob lowered the volume on the radio and idled his truck up to the service window at the Emerson border crossing. The banks of fluorescent lights washed out the color of the pavement. Away from the crossing and the segregated lanes, the world became lost in darkness. Two lanes down, a tractor trailer pulled away, leaving Jacob's as the only vehicle on the northbound side.

The border agent leaned forward with one hand extended from the giant glass box. A sleeve of dark tattoos spanned from his wrist to the cuff of his shirt. His thinning hair had a hint of gray at the temples. "Welcome to Canada. What brings you through at this hour?"

Jacob turned the ignition off, pushed the rolled cuffs of his plaid cotton shirt up his forearms, and dragged a backpack to his side. "Just going home. I mean, I'm coming home." From inside the pack, he pulled out his Canadian passport, then scooped up his license from the seat between his legs and held both out to the agent.

As the agent pulled the documents back, Jacob focused on

a distended face on his arm. It was little more than a corpse, but had vivid eyes. The agent adjusted his glasses and scanned Jacob's information. "Home, you say? Looks like you're headed in the wrong direction." He raised an eyebrow and held up a South Dakota driver's license.

"Oh, right." He looked through the back window to the bed of the truck. "I still have my Ontario license. Somewhere. Things didn't work out the way I thought."

The corners of the border agent's mouth turned down. "I'm sorry to hear that." He swiveled in his chair and typed at his keyboard. "Could I also see your registration and proof of insurance, please?"

"Oh, sure." Jacob leaned over and opened the glove box. He took out the small plastic folder and handed it over.

"You have a place to stay?"

"Yeah, I mean, I think so."

"And where would that be, exactly?"

"Fort Erie."

The agent leaned over and scanned the box of Jacob's truck as he picked at his teeth with his tongue. "Any firearms, ammunition, or other weapons in the vehicle?"

"No, Sir."

"Drugs, cannabis, or related products?"

"No."

"Anything to declare? Goods? Funds over ten thousand dollars?"

"Afraid not. I barely got out with a change of clothes."

The border agent shook his head. "It was like that, was it?"

Jacob frowned and rubbed at his eye. "Unfortunately."

The clicking resumed for a moment. It ended with an exuberant stab at the return key. After two sharp snaps of a stamp, the agent leaned against the window frame and held Jacob's license and passport out. "Do me a favor. Take the first right up ahead, follow it across the river, then take the next left. Motel is a block in. Someone'll be at the desk. Get some rest. The road will still be there in the morning."

Jacob pursed his lips into a faint smile. "Thanks."

The agent nodded and turned back to his computer. "Welcome home, Mr. Dalstrom."

TWO

Jacob woke with the dawn. He pushed stiff sheets off his body, stood, and shuffled into the bathroom. The space was clean but cramped. A single lightbulb cast unforgiving white light. The beige textured wallpaper curled in the corners and bubbled at the seams. In the middle of the mottled-brown laminate counter sat a small hand sink, with his wallet and keys beside.

With one eye open, Jacob leaned over the toilet and released the pressure from his bladder. The elastic on his boxers snapped as he pulled them up. He let out a slow exhale and reached out to flush.

When he turned toward the mirror over the sink, he kept his eyes low. He took one of the glasses from the corner of the counter and peeled off the paper cap. Filled to the rim, he drank it down, then refilled and drained it a second time. With the empty glass pushed to one side, he wiped at his mouth with the back of his hand.

Jacob kicked his underwear off as he turned toward the shower. Once in the tub, he pulled the thin plastic curtain across. He recoiled at the crooked stream of icy water, but as it warmed, he moved closer to the shower head and wiped water over his face and down his arms. Jacob stretched out against the wall and tucked his chin, letting the warmth run down his neck and back. The aches and stress began to ease.

He reached out for soap that wasn't there, then cleared the water from his eyes and pushed the curtain back. With one foot on the cold tile floor, he reached for the bar of soap on the countertop. The paper wrapper fell to the floor. He pulled his leg back in and slid the curtain closed. A sharp chemical smell filled his lungs when he held the soap under the flowing water. He squeezed it, then lathered himself from head to toe.

When he finished, Jacob set the sliver that remained on the side of the tub. A familiar tackiness came over his skin as he rinsed himself clean. Jacob turned the water off and reached out past the curtain for a towel hanging on the wall, draped the thin rectangle of fabric on top of his head and worked it over his hair and face. Without doing much else, he wrapped it around his waist, pushed the curtain back, and stepped out of the tub.

Water dripped onto the tiles around his feet in a light patter. He stared at the vague shape in the fogged mirror and felt some small sense of connection. A man with no face or identity. The stink of days and years past now washed away. Maybe, he thought, it was a good enough place to start. His life could be whatever he wanted it to be. Jacob sniffed. He ran a hand through his damp red hair, long on top, shaved close at the sides, and walked back into the room.

His backpack laid open on the end of the bed, a duffle bag on the floor beside it. Jacob sat on one squeaky corner of the mattress and loosened the towel over his legs. He pulled the backpack close and sorted through the contents. His hand grazed something hard underneath the hastily packed clothes. Jacob paused, then wrapped his fingers around the object and pulled it out.

He held the wooden box in his palm. Dark stain pooled in the ridges of the rose design carved on the top. A half-forgotten memory played in his mind as he ran a hand over the lid. The smell of fresh cut black walnut, the feel of the chisel in his hand, and the proud look on his grandfather's face.

Jacob slipped off two ink-stained elastic bands from around the box and flipped the lid back. The box was packed to the brim with his past, some distant, some more recent. He sorted through memorabilia from the places he lived growing up. A pin and a special looking rock. On the bottom, he found a handmade bookmark that Wendy McInnon gave him when they were twelve years old. Wendy was his first love. He would likely never forget her, or at least the feeling of that time, but so much else had been lost from his memory.

Jacob brought out a small rolled up brown paper bag and set it beside him, then picked up a worn blue velvet ring box in the palm of his hand. He eased the top of the ring box open and watched the single small diamond bend the glow from the overhead light. The ring had been his grandmother's. It was one of two items that Jacob acquired after his grandparents passed away the year before. He knew it may not have been Charlotte's style, being shy on carats and design, but he had hoped it would have been enough.

Charlotte.

Her name pulsed in his mind. His body ached, but not from any sort of physical discomfort. Echoes of coming home to his belongings strewn across the front lawn, the angry words hurled at him as the neighbors looked on, all flashed across his mind. He pushed them away as a tear broke loose from the corner of his eye.

Jacob set the ring aside, then unrolled the brown paper bag and let the contents drop onto his lap. He did not need to count it. The thick roll of bills totaled just shy of four thousand dollars. Jacob had been setting aside money for the last three years so he could take Charlotte on her dream honeymoon to Hawaii. Now, the money would allow some sort of new start. He slipped out a few bills and dropped them on his wallet, then set everything else back inside the wooden box, secured the lid, and put it in his pack.

Jacob flipped his wallet open and slid the money in. He eyed the debit and credit cards before pulling them out. The previous twenty-four hours proved to be some of the most difficult in recent memory. Getting locked out of his account —their bank accounts, he reminded himself—had been but one of the highlights. Jacob folded the cards in half with shaking hands, then flicked them toward the small open garbage can beside the TV.

The coffee maker gurgled and dripped while Jacob dressed and packed. He made a final check of the room as he drank the bitter, dark liquid. On paper, he had managed longer days with less sleep, but the weight added by his current situation was yet to be known.

———

Jacob slid through the closing convenience store door with two large bottles of water tucked under one arm, and a handful of change along with directions to the nearest laundromat in his hand. He walked into the late morning sun, hanging lazy over Winnipeg's skyline, past empty gas station lanes, to his truck parked at the far pump.

He set the water on the front seat, then confirmed the prepayment had registered at the pump. As he lifted the nozzle, squealing tires came from the street. An older four-door Mercedes Benz, with oversized rims and a thumping stereo, sped up to the set of pumps over from Jacob. The music and engine silenced, but the commotion inside continued. A woman in a black hoodie exited from the passenger side and stormed off toward the store. The driver's door flew open and a man, a few years younger than Jacob, emerged. Dark slicked down hair fanned out at the back. The arms of his tight-fitting jean jacket rolled up to his elbows. He pulled mirror tinted sunglasses from his face and leaned over top of the car. "You're lucky I don't leave your ass right here. Stupid bitch."

The man kicked the car door closed as he turned to the pump, then he caught Jacob's gaze. "What's your problem?"

Jacob lowered his eyes and shook his head.

"Yeah, that's what I thought, fuckin' punk." He kicked the door closed and muttered to himself as he fished his wallet from his back pocket.

Jacob's pump slowed and clicked off shy of a full tank. He slipped the nozzle back into its holder and sat in the truck. After a quick look to the man in the Benz, he leaned forward and searched for street signs. He decided on a direction, started the truck, then drove out to the road.

———

Half melted snow scattered across the shoulders and the ditches, but the road out of Winnipeg stayed clear for the most part. Jacob dialed in a classic rock station on the radio and settled back in the seat. He set his right hand on top of the steering wheel, and his left arm rested on his raised knee. He drove on that way, without looking back.

After crossing into Kenora, Jacob detoured onto Highway 17 to go through town. He had never been before and wanted to stretch his legs. Jacob pulled the truck into a roadside plaza and parked on the west side. He opened his door, stepped out, and reached his arms high over his head with hands clasped in a shuddering stretch.

He wandered past the building, through a band of ragged trees, and out toward a glimmer of water a short distance to the north. He stopped at a set of dual lane train tracks and put a hand down to the cold metal rails. He did not feel anything, so he walked toward a narrow line of trees marking the edge of the Lake of the Woods. Thin patches of ice formed at the edges of the calm water. Jacob warmed his hands in his coat pockets, his right hand wrapped around his cell phone. He realized it had been almost twenty-four hours since he looked at it, so with a held breath, he drew it from his pocket and pressed the power button. The phone lit up and buzzed as notifications stacked on the screen.

Jacob tapped on the message icon and scrolled through line after line of harsh words and ill will. He expected it from Charlotte's family, but not from the people he considered his friends.

How could you do this to her?

Rot in hell.

From Charlotte's uncle simply—*you're fired.*

Charlotte had sent a single note. *Check ur messages.*

Jacob closed the messenger app and touched the lit-up voicemail icon. He deleted most after hearing the first few words, but he stopped at the sound of Charlotte's voice, calm and subdued. Jacob closed his eyes.

"Jacob, it's me. I just want to make myself perfectly clear. We're done. I'm tired of your lies. I'm tired of waiting for you to step up and be a man. I don't know what I ever did to make you treat me this way, but I'm not putting up with it anymore. Mama was right about you. I only wish I'd seen it sooner. Don't call me, don't text me, and don't call *my* friends. I've made sure everyone knows what you've done. Don't ever show your face around here again."

He stared at his phone, chin trembling. Jacob screamed out as fresh tears came. He brought his arm back and threw the phone with all the force he could muster. With the ripples on the surface of the lake expanding, he turned and stormed back across the tracks.

Emerging into the parking lot, Jacob tripped on a dead branch but recovered at the last second. He watched the ground, hands clenched by his side and his teeth grinding, doing his best to ignore the concerned glances from people passing to and from their vehicles. He wiped cold tears away as he arrived at the truck. Once behind the wheel, he slammed the door. With his head low, he pressed the heels of his hands against his eyes.

Jacob knew how Charlotte could be. If he thought about it, none of what happened should have been a surprise. The jealous and irrational side of her had always been just under the surface. In that moment, it hit him that he had uprooted his life and moved to another country for no good reason. It hurt more than he knew it could.

He stared out of the windshield while drawing short breaths, watching the branches of the trees sway, and the clouds change shape in the sky. Jacob adjusted in his seat and brought himself close to the rear-view mirror. He ran a hand down his face and cleared his throat, then buckled in and started the engine.

———

Outside of Vermilion Bay, the music faded into garbled words and static. Tired of contemporary commercial radio, Jacob pressed the seek button. With the only options being talk radio and religious programming, he gave it a rest instead.

The sound of a howling engine came before the car rounded the corner ahead. High beams glaring, and doing at least thirty over the limit, it passed by in a streak of silver. Jacob glimpsed taillights in the rear-view before they disappeared.

Past the first river bridge, he spotted someone walking along the side of the road. Jacob eased off the accelerator and straightened his back. An oversized black hoodie masked her figure like a cloak. Ratty jeans soaked halfway to her knee, and the laces on her dirt-stained running shoes fell loose. She adjusted the bag slung over her shoulder. As he scanned her features, recognition dawned. It was the woman from the gas station.

She held her hand low with her thumb out toward the road. A large brindle dog, with white patches on its chest and feet, sat by her side. Its ears perked as Jacob drifted by.

The pain he saw radiating from the woman's vibrant, sable eyes felt familiar. Jacob made a quick check to the road behind and pulled to the shoulder. Frigid air brushed his face when he lowered the passenger side window. He turned in his seat to watch the pair as they ambled up alongside the truck.

The woman watched Jacob but did not speak.

Jacob looked back along the road. "Was that…"

"Yeah."

"Umm, so where are you two headed?"

She motioned with her head. "East."

"Well, that's where I'm heading. I'm hoping to make it to Thunder Bay before I stop for the night."

The woman watched Jacob for a moment, then broke her eyes away. "You from South Dakota?" Her voice sounded hoarse, like someone who had been awake for too long.

Jacob paused and squinted. "Oh," he shook his head, "no, not anymore."

"You're not a rapist or anything, are you?"

"I…no. Definitely not."

The woman faced Jacob, but her eyes still focused elsewhere. "I have a knife. The dog will rip your throat out if you touch me."

"Fair enough."

She appeared to consider the situation, then nodded. "Okay."

She turned and walked to the back of the truck. The dog fell in beside her. Jacob watched in the mirror as she dropped the tailgate and hopped up to sit on it. She patted her hand on the gate, and the dog jumped up into the box. The woman wrapped her arms around the dog and buried her face in its back. "Be good." She hopped to the ground and lifted the tailgate shut.

The woman took her bag by the strap and slid a hand along the top of the box as she walked up the side of the truck. With her fingers resting on the handle, she hesitated, watching Jacob without emotion. "Remember what I said before, right?"

"Something about a knife and losing my throat?"

"Yeah."

"I remember."

The woman climbed into the truck and pulled her sweater up over her mouth. She shrank into the far corner of the seat with both arms wrapped around the bag on her lap. The cab filled with the smell of damp denim. Strands of russet hair hung and obscured her face. Her full cheeks held a red tinge from the cold.

"Seatbelt?"

"I'm good."

Jacob raised his eyebrows. "Okay."

Jacob craned his neck to look back. The dog sat up tall with its tongue hanging from one side of its mouth. It looked from Jacob to its human, with one clear blue eye and one golden brown. Jacob checked the driver's side mirror, put the truck into gear, and pulled back onto the highway.

As they got up to speed, the woman opened the sliding back window. A large square head poked through, and the woman's left hand came up to scratch under the dog's jaw. It responded with a low, contented groan.

"What's his name?"

"Her name is Sam. Like Samantha."

"Oh. Sorry. Have you had her long?"

"Since she was a puppy."

"Nice. What kind of dog is she?"

"Not sure. A mutt."

"I've heard they're the best kind to have."

The woman shrugged and looked away.

They continued in silence for some time. Jacob flexed his fingers around the wheel and swallowed. With everything else going on, he wondered why he stopped. The idea of being pulled over with a stranger in his truck, not knowing what she had on her or what drama she might bring, held little appeal.

He pushed back in his seat. "I'm Jacob, by the way."

The woman watched him for a moment, then lowered her chin and tucked her hands into her sleeves. "Hi, Jacob."

"What do I call you?"

The woman focused forward.

"Listen, really, you don't need to worry." Jacob gave an awkward smile.

The woman watched him from the corner of her eye. "Mati."

"Pardon?"

"M.A.T.I. Mati."

"Oh. Right. Nice to officially meet you, Mati." Jacob searched around in the plastic shopping bag on the seat beside him. "Hey, would you like some gum?"

Mati stared at him, her face like stone.

Jacob flushed. "Oh, no. I mean, not that you need it. I was just, you know…"

"No, thanks."

Jacob cleared his throat. "Sorry." He turned the radio on and the volume up, then focused on the road.

———

Jacob stopped at the first gas station he could find in Ignace. Mati went to the back of the truck and sat on the tailgate with Sam. Walking to the pump, Jacob turned to look along the road. The sun rested low on the horizon. Streetlights flickered and lit up. He put the nozzle in the filler, pulled back on the handle, and set the lock. He fished out a bottle of motor oil from a crate in the bed of the truck, then went up and popped the hood. The dipstick showed the oil a little low, but not bad. He added a third of the bottle to the engine, then put it back in the bed of the truck.

Jacob paused and scratched at the back of his neck. He turned at the sound of shuffling feet across the lot. Four men stood at the side of the convenience store near a blue dumpster. They wore heavy boots, dirty jeans, and tattered flannel jackets. Dark eyes peered out from under the brims of their caps. One had a lit cigarette rolling back and forth between his fingertips. He kept a close eye on the truck. Jacob looked to Mati. Her eyes searched, but she kept her head low.

One of the men turned sideways and muttered to his friend. Jacob could not hear over the distance and the humming of the pump. The one with the cigarette smiled and hung the butt from the corner of his mouth. He tapped his friend on the chest with the back of his hand before walking into the shadows.

Jacob flinched when the pump snapped off. He tilted his head back and rolled his eyes. "Jesus." Jacob holstered the nozzle. "Maybe you should get in the truck. I'll be right back."

Mati hopped down and latched the tailgate.

Jacob ran through the door of the convenience store, dropped a stack of bills on the counter, and dashed back. He buckled his seatbelt and looked to the now vacant space in front of the dumpster.

"It's okay. They're gone."

"Good. Probably nothing, right?"

Mati crossed her arms. "Maybe."

Jacob let out a slow exhale and started the engine. "I could use something to eat, but we can keep going if you think that's better."

Mati focused out the side window.

"I'll buy. I think you've dealt with enough today."

Mati gave Jacob a skewed look and turned in her seat to scan the line of businesses in the immediate vicinity. "How far to the next town?"

"About half an hour, I think."

Focusing halfway up the block, Mati gave an upward nod. "Pizza is fine."

"Sure, sounds good."

Jacob took a right turn out of the gas station lot, and at the next intersection, spun the truck around to park outside of the pizza shop's big front window. Jacob and Mati walked up to the entrance. Sam stood in the bed of the truck, front feet on the arched wheel well, with her ears perked. Mati held up a finger. "Stay, Sam."

Sam licked at her lips and backed down.

A bell on the door chimed when Jacob and Mati entered. The warm aroma of baking dough and melting cheese greeted them inside. A voice called out from the back. "Grab a seat. I'll be with you in a minute."

The furniture was typical of a small town diner. Laminate tabletops with wood trim and black pedestal bases lined the perimeter. The linoleum floor showed wear marks from when the tables had once been positioned closer together. Jacob and Mati each pulled out a red vinyl chair from a table by the front window and sat. Jacob took a menu from between a bottle of ketchup and a chili shaker. He set it down sideways in the middle of the table. "What do you like?"

"Pepperoni is fine. Need some for Sam too, if that's okay."

A middle-aged woman came out of the back, wiping her hands on a white cloth tucked into the string of her apron. Her shaggy auburn hair was tied back in a hasty ponytail, and perspiration beaded on her brow. Bright green eyes and her wide smile made Jacob feel welcome. "Sorry about that, guys, just finishing up a takeout order. You've had a look at the menu? What can I get for you?"

"Can we get a large pepperoni, please? I'll take a large cola as well. Whatever you have is fine."

"Perfect. Anything for you, sweetie?"

"Iced tea. Please."

"Sounds good, be right back."

Jacob gave a thin smile. "Thanks."

Jacob and Mati sat alone with the hum of the beverage cooler behind the counter and the faint rhythm of an oldies station playing in the kitchen.

"So…" Jacob brushed his hands down his pant legs. "What happened? You being left on the side of the road and all."

"I don't know. I have shitty taste in men?"

Jacob nodded with thin lips. "Uh, where were you guys…I mean, where are you going?"

Mati stretched and rested her forearms on the edge of the table. She played with the tattered cuffs of her sleeves. "Montréal. I'm going to see my dad."

"Oh. Nice."

The owner of the restaurant walked to the table with a large plastic tumbler in each hand. "Here you go, guys. Pizza won't be long."

Jacob smiled. "Thanks."

Mati watched the woman go back behind the counter and into the kitchen, then she stared back at her hands.

"We'll see. He doesn't know I'm coming."

"Is Montréal home?"

"No." Mati focused on her iced tea.

"Oh…"

Jacob watched out the front window but saw little of interest. Few cars drove past as most people had settled at home for the evening. Sam kept an eye on something up the street.

Mati broke the quiet. "What about you? What are you running from?"

Jacob let out a short burst of a laugh, but there was no real humor in it. "I don't know. I'm trying to focus on what I'm running to, not from."

"Did you kill someone?"

"What? No."

"So, it's a girl then."

Jacob's hand tightened around his glass.

"What's her name?"

Jacob cleared his throat. "Charlotte."

"Nice name."

"I suppose."

Mati watched Jacob. He refused to meet her gaze. They sat in silence until the pizza arrived.

Mati devoured two slices for every one that Jacob did. When they finished, Jacob asked to package up the last few slices to go. He settled the bill, said goodbye to the owner, and followed Mati out into the cool night air.

Sam wiggled and hopped as Mati dropped the tailgate and sat beside her. Mati ran a hand down the coarse hair on her back while she choked down the leftovers, then pulled a clear bottle from her bag and poured it into her hand for Sam to lap up. When she had her fill, Mati wrapped her arms around Sam's neck and squeezed. "Good girl."

Mati dropped to the asphalt. With the gate secured, she

took her spot in the passenger seat. Jacob sat ready behind the wheel.

"So, we're still good to try for Thunder Bay?"

"Yeah." Mati fixed her gaze on the floor. "Thanks. For the pizza."

Jacob smiled. "No problem at all." He put the truck in gear, and they continued east.

———

Darkness settled. Jacob kept the music low, but they rarely spoke. Mati had finished off a bag of nachos with a little help from Sam. Sleep found her twenty minutes outside of Thunder Bay. The strain of almost twelve hours on the road settled over Jacob. He tilted his head back and forth to stretch out the tension in his neck and yawned. Driving the city streets, he searched for a decent place to spend the night.

Jacob settled on a small motel on the north-east side of town, bordering Lake Superior. A large, flashy sign outside boasted "Colour TV" along with "Free WiFi". More importantly, the neon vacancy sign glowed bright. Jacob drove the truck into the uneven asphalt parking lot and killed the engine.

Mati's eyes went wide, and her jaw clenched. She looked around and stifled a yawn before her body relaxed. "Where are we?"

"Thunder Bay. Just pulled into the motel."

"Oh." Mati stretched and began collecting her things. She avoided eye contact as she got out of the truck. At the back of the bed, she dropped the gate and called to Sam. "Come on."

Sam jumped down to the pavement and sniffed around for a spot to relieve herself. Mati started toward the main road, but she paused a few steps in and turned halfway around. "Can I ride with you again tomorrow?"

"Of course."

"When are you leaving?"

"I don't know, probably around eight."

"Okay."

"Looks like it's going to be cold tonight. I can get you a room if you want."

Mati raised her eyes, then she turned to walk away. "I can take care of myself."

"Okay." Jacob lowered his head and moved on toward the motel office.

THREE

Deep, resonant barking shook Jacob from his fitful sleep. Bleary eyed, he grabbed the alarm clock on the nightstand. Red numerals read three thirty-seven. Jacob sat up and hunched forward. Nothing good happens after three o'clock in the morning. From the window, he watched snow skim across the ground and fog hover at the edge of the lake. As his eyes adjusted, he spotted Sam in the middle of the parking lot. Mati laid motionless on the ground a short distance away.

Jacob slipped his pants and boots on before he snatched a room key from beside the TV and bolted out the door. He slid on the dusting of snow as he knelt beside Mati. Sam wagged her tail, and her ears dropped back.

Jacob grabbed Mati's shoulders and gently shook them. "Mati. *Mati.*"

Her eyes fluttered. She mouthed a few words, but little sound emerged.

Jacob spotted Mati's bag near the curb, so dashed over to grab it and toss it in the back of his truck, before he returned to Mati and wove an arm under her shoulders and one under her knees. With a groan, he lifted her and shuffled back to his room with Sam on his heels.

He propped Mati up against the frame and fumbled with the key to open the door. Inside, he laid her down on the nearest bed. Sam slipped into the room right before the door slammed shut. Jacob pulled off Mati's wet boots and socks, then wrapped the comforter over her. Sam jumped up on the bed and laid down beside her.

The smell of alcohol and acrid smoke overwhelmed Jacob. He grabbed an empty water bottle from the dresser and took it to the bathroom to fill. On his way back, he stopped to turn the thermostat up. He sat on the bed and put a hand under Mati's head.

"Mati. Come on, wake up. You need to drink."

Mati's eyes moved side to side under closed lids.

Jacob brought the bottle to Mati's lips. "Drink." She managed a couple short sips before losing her strength.

Jacob knew what fall down drunk looked like. Whatever Mati was experiencing went well beyond that. He shook her shoulder. "Come on, wake up. Tell me what happened."

Mati turned her head and mumbled through tight lips. "Fine. I'm fine."

"Jesus…" Jacob stood and laced his fingers on the top of his head. He scanned the room, searching for direction.

"S'okay," Mati turned her head away. "Sleep."

Jacob got her to drink more water, then stripped the top blanket from the other bed and draped it over her. He moved a chair up beside her and slumped down with his arms crossed over his bare chest. He monitored Mati's ragged breathing until the rising sun lit up the curtains drawn across the motel room window.

———

Jacob opened his eyes, finding it hard to focus at first. Everything hurt, though his back and neck screamed the loudest. The clock beside the bed showed a quarter to ten.

Mati bolted upright. She looked around the room as she pulled the blankets up to her neck.

Jacob sat forward. "You okay?"

"Think so."

"What the hell happened?"

Mati kept her head down and scratched Sam's ear. "Just looking for something to do. Got in with some people I shouldn't have. It happens."

"It happens? How the hell does that just happen?"

"Can we talk later? Not feeling too good." Mati finished the last of the water from the bottle on the bedside table, then laid back and pulled the blankets over her head.

"Guess so." Jacob leaned forward and rubbed at the back of his neck. He stood and picked up his bag on the way to the bathroom. He brushed his teeth and took a ninety-second hot shower before he dressed and came back into the room.

"I'm going to get some breakfast. Be ready to go in half an hour, or I'm leaving without you."

Mati pulled the blankets just below her eyes. "Have you seen my bag?"

Jacob raised a thumb over his shoulder. "Back off the truck."

Mati nodded and disappeared again.

Walking to the door, Jacob stubbed his toe on the bed frame. He swore under his breath. Sam's head popped up. Mati did not move. Jacob put on his coat and boots and let the door click shut behind him.

The shock of the cool morning air stole Jacob's breath. He pulled his coat tight around his body and jogged to the truck. He let the engine idle as he waited for the frost on the windshield to relent. When he could see well enough, he drove out of the parking lot, and up the street, to a drive-thru he had noticed the night before. He pulled up to order and waited for the food with his window halfway down. On his way back, he stopped to fill up the truck and grab a few snacks for the road.

Jacob pushed through the door of the motel room, with two large bags in one hand and a four-cup tray in the other. Mati sat on the edge of the bed drying her hair. She stole a quick look at Jacob but saw the venom in his eyes and diverted her attention.

"There's orange juice and coffee. Breakfast sandwiches are in the bag. I want to be on the road in fifteen minutes."

"Okay. Almost done."

Jacob exhaled and sat on the opposite bed. He tore open one bag of food, unwrapped a breakfast sandwich, and took two large bites. Warm coffee washed it down.

Neither spoke a word while they ate or when they packed up to leave. Mati and Sam waited at the back of the truck until Jacob returned from checking out.

Mati stood with her arms crossed. "Am I still okay to ride with you?"

Jacob shrugged. "As long as you keep the drama to an acceptable level."

Mati shrugged. "I can just go…"

"If that's what you think is best."

They watched each other until Mati looked away.

Jacob sighed. "I'll be in the truck."

He started the engine, set the radio, and unwrapped a

piece of gum. When he looked in the mirror, Mati leaned against the side of the bed with her hood up, holding herself. She wiped at her eyes and dropped the gate. Sam jumped up and settled at the top of the box. Mati latched the gate, shook it to be sure, then took her spot in the passenger seat.

Jacob drove onto Hodder Avenue toward the Trans-Canada Highway. Mati watched Lake Superior fade away to her right. She pushed the hood of her sweater back and turned to face Jacob. Fresh tears welled in her eyes. "I'm sorry about last night. I didn't mean to drag you into my mess."

Jacob offered an awkward smile. "It's okay. I'm glad you're all right."

Mati's lips quivered, but she managed to return the gesture before turning back to the side window. "Things haven't been easy for me lately. I really need a change, and my dad is all I've got left. It's…I don't know, stressful."

Jacob nodded. "I get it. It's okay."

The sun glared off roadside puddles as they passed and provided gentle warmth through the windows. Mati stifled a yawn. She propped her bag up against the door and leaned into it. Jacob settled in and put his foot down, doing his best to make up some time without getting into trouble.

———

Mati yawned and stretched as Jacob pulled the truck into a gas station outside of Wawa. "What time is it?"

"Just after five. How are you feeling?"

"Thirsty."

"I think there's a bottle of water left in the bag there. I'll grab some more, just in case."

"It's okay, I'll get some. I've got to go to the bathroom anyway."

Jacob pumped gas while Mati walked inside. He topped off the tank as she returned with a large bottle of water and two bags of nachos balanced in her arms. She went to the back of the truck and released the tailgate. She cracked the lid and guzzled down half the bottle. She poured the rest of the water into her hand so Sam could drink.

"I need to take her for a bathroom break. Be right back."

"No problem. I'll be here."

Mati and Sam strolled around the south side of the building. Jacob went through the door and straight to the bathroom. After cleaning up, he roamed the aisles, loading his arms with pop and bottles of water.

Jacob came back to the truck, snacks in tow. Mati leaned forward on the tailgate with her fingers wrapped around the edge. Sam sniffed at a patchy strip of grass by the median.

"Dinner on the road okay?"

"Sure."

"It's going to make for a long day, but I want to get to Sudbury before stopping for the night."

Mati nodded. "Okay."

———

Cold air, blistering out of the north, kicked up debris along the side of the highway. Jacob followed well behind a line of slow-moving traffic.

Mati looked to Jacob from the corner of her eye. "Tell me a story."

Jacob raised an eyebrow. "A story? What do you mean?"

"Not sure." Mati squinted. "Tell me about Charlotte."

"Oh, man." Jacob scratched at his forehead before running his hand back to smooth out his hair. "It's a bit of a long story."

Mati twisted in her seat and leaned back against the door. "I've got time."

Jacob frowned. "What do you want to know?"

"How you got here. Start at the beginning."

"Right." He adjusted his grip on the steering wheel. "Well, I was working construction in Toronto, living with my best friend, Evan. We were invited out one Friday to see a new band. I think his girlfriend knew the lead singer or something.

"I took the wrong bus and got lost, was almost an hour late. None of that mattered after I walked into the bar and saw Charlotte. She was a sophomore at the University of Toronto, working toward her bachelor's degree in Agriculture and Bio-Resources. She grew up in Hartford, just outside of Sioux Falls, in South Dakota. Her dad had plans for her to become the fourth generation to take on the family business. Charlotte used to say that going to school in Toronto was her opportunity to have some fun before that happened."

Jacob gave a sad smile and checked his mirrors. "I won't ever forget the first time we were alone. Sort of alone, anyway. She asked me to stop by and see her at work. It was this hipster gift shop in Old Town. I just remember a bunch of Edison bulbs, painted mason jars, and birdhouses made from old license plates. We talked for hours, not sure about what. And that's all it took. From then on, she had me wrapped around her little finger.

"After Charlotte graduated, I moved home with her so we could be together. Her Uncle Duncan owns a trucking company and had a job waiting for me. Her mom found us a place to live, too. It just happened to be right across the street from her house.

"At first, things were great. That didn't last long, though. Charlotte got upset when I went out with the guys. She made a habit of checking up on me all the time and going through my messages.

"Duncan was a bit of a hard ass. Didn't think much of me either. As soon as the opportunity came up, he moved me from local routes to long haul. I needed a job to stay, so I stuck it out. Being gone all the time made life at home less than fun. Long story short, three days ago, I came home to everything I own out on the front lawn. So, here I am."

Mati lowered her head and focused on her hands. "I'm sorry."

Jacob swallowed against the hitch in his throat. "It is what it is."

Mati nodded and looked out at the blurred landscape as they drove on.

———

Mati sat close to the window and watched the sky as they passed the Sudbury city limits sign. Jacob pulled into the first motel he saw. The brick façade was dirty, chipped in places. Wiry, overgrown shrubs lined the entrance. Half the lights in the sign out front had burned out. Anxious to get some rest, he was not in the mood to be picky. He parked in a free spot near the office, opened his door, then turned back to Mati. "Don't move."

Mati's eyes darted between Jacob and the floor of the cab. "Okay."

She chewed her nails as Jacob shuffled into the motel

office. Her focus moved between the clock on the dash and the office door. Seconds felt like minutes, and minutes like hours. Mati tensed when Jacob appeared again.

He grabbed his backpack and duffle bag from the bed of the truck, then collected what remained of the food. "Room one-twelve. Once Sam has done her business, put her in the cab. You can sneak her up later." Jacob closed the door and walked away.

When Mati arrived at the room, a phonebook propped the door open. She slipped inside and nudged the book out of the way with her foot. Jacob laid on the bed furthest from the door, arms and legs spread to the corners. His feet hung off the end, boots and all. Jacob raised his head as Mati entered. Sam sniffed at the floor behind her.

"It's okay, nobody saw us."

Jacob frowned. "Did you lock the truck?"

"Yeah."

"Okay." Jacob closed his eyes and lowered his head to the pillow.

Mati sat cross-legged on the end of the empty bed. Sam hopped up and laid down beside her. Both bed side lamps were on but did little to illuminate the small room. Sparse and dingy walls held up the warped, moisture-stained ceiling. The dark pattern in the carpet showed clearly worn paths and questionable sticky spots of unknown origin. The furniture came from a different generation, made with dark woodgrain laminate and bolt-together construction. The tube TV was an interesting touch. Mati thought it gave the place the feel of a bad eighties' horror movie. Thankfully, the sheets were clean, and the beds appeared comfortable enough.

Mati flinched when Jacob started talking into his pillow. "I'm going to get up now. Then, I'm going to shower. After that, I'm going to sleep. I feel the need to mention that you are welcome to stay. I may snore a little, but otherwise, you're safe here. Feel free to go if you think that's best."

Jacob rose, stiff and off balance. "There's a spare key on the TV, in case you need to go out. You know, if you're staying." He shuffled into the bathroom. A long, painful groan came from the open door, and a pair of boots flung out into the room. The door closed, and the shower shuttered to life. Mati sat on the bed, running her hand over Sam's head. She glanced toward the exit and frowned.

———

After showering, Jacob sorted through his backpack. He pulled out a clean pair of underwear, a pair of shorts, and a shirt. He dressed, then arranged his toiletries on the counter.

Jacob raised his hand to wipe the condensation from the mirror, but stopped. A faint outline of a heart framed his blurred reflection. Remnants of letters, a name perhaps, filled the middle. The forgotten gesture of affection brought his own situation rushing back to the forefront of his mind. He swiped his flattened hand across the mirror, back and forth, in an attempt to push both away.

Jacob readied his toothbrush, then worked it in slow, circular motions as he studied his pale face and the heavy bags under his eyes. The freckles on his cheeks stood out more than usual. He felt compelled to shave, but it was a reaction to a memory, an old routine still picking at the back of his mind. Brush hanging from his mouth, he leaned in toward the mirror. He scratched at the scar on his chin, the one Charlotte gave him. Proof, at least, of what he had been through. Other wounds resided in places that could not be seen. Jacob spit, rinsed, and shuffled back into the room with his dirty clothes balled up in his hand.

Mati's hoodie hung over the end of the bed closest to the door. Sam stretched out, resting her head on it. Her half-closed eyes tracked Jacob as he walked across the room. Mati had buried herself in a lump under the sheets. Jacob grew concerned that it was some kind of decoy until the gentle rise and fall showed her shallow breath. Jacob moved toward the door to set the locks, but Mati already latched the deadbolt and drew the chain. He turned and made his way up between the two beds.

"Night, Sam."

Jacob flipped the sheets back on his bed and sat. Dirty clothes dropped down on the far side of the bed, then he slid his wallet and watch under his pillow. Jacob reached over, turned off both bedside lamps, and slipped under the sheets. Within moments, he fell fast asleep.

FOUR

Alex hunched over and hung his head while he twisted a half-empty beer bottle. He showed no interest in the pounding rhythm shaking the air, or the surging mass of bodies on the dance floor. He was an anomaly in the otherwise boisterous room. His jacket stayed zipped to the collar, the Velcro cuffs wrapped tight. A grayed-out American flag on his shoulder was the only visible variation from the matte black polyester shell.

The blonde next to him steadied herself against the bar. Even without the glittery stilettos, he would have had to look up to make eye contact with her. She smiled and held her hips at just the right angle, but not in his direction. "So, why do they call you Taz?"

The man's smile was all teeth, except for the gap in the middle. He leaned in, his dark eyes flecked with gold. "It's 'cause of the Tasmanian Devil, right? That's what I'm like in the bedroom. I tear shit up…"

The blonde squealed.

Taz tilted back and laughed at the exposed ceiling.

Alex looked away and muttered to himself. "Holy shit…"

Taz set a hand on the blonde's waist and moved in to whisper in her ear. She squealed again, feigned to move away, then fell in closer.

Alex lifted his beer to his lips. It missed the mark when his torso pushed forward into the bar. He scowled, set the bottle down, and turned. A man, with heavy eyes and a crooked smile, stood with his arms out. Someone behind him, Alex assumed his handler, pulled on one sleeve while keeping their attention elsewhere.

"Sorry, man. This is my *jam*." The man made a few uncoordinated twists of his body and faded into the crowd.

Alex returned to his beer and drained it. He looked to Taz, but the big man had locked onto the blonde like a heat seeking missile. Alex nodded to the bartender while holding up his empty bottle, then crossed his arms and leaned forward.

Alex reached out when a new bottle appeared. Behind him, the song changed. A bachelorette and her friends screamed in excitement. The packed dance floor swarmed as multi-colored lights flashed across the walls. Again, Alex's body jolted forward. His fingers grazed the top of the bottle and knocked it on its side. Beer flowed and foamed across the bar top and dripped down to the floor. He pushed back from the bar to avoid the spray. A hand rested on his shoulder, and a slurred voice sounded next to his ear. "Sorry, man. Real sorry."

Heat rushed through Alex's temples. He spun around, teeth grinding, in time to see the drunk man stumbled backward. The friend once again came to his side. Alex pointed a finger. "Last chance. Got it?"

The friend held out a hand. "Come on, it's his birthday. He's just having a little fun."

"*Last. Chance.*"

"Okay, okay." The friend pulled the drunk into the crowd.

Alex ran a hand through his hair. His cheeks puffed out as he exhaled. "*Taz.*"

Taz broke away from the blonde. "Wha?"

"I'm gonna make a call."

Taz shot him a thumbs-up.

Alex pulled down on the zipper at his collar, then adjusted the ring of fabric pooled around his neck up over his nose. As he walked away, the blonde took his spot.

On his way out the door, Alex bumped a fist with the bouncer, then walked along the line of green taxis to the next streetlight. He took his phone from the zippered pocket of his jacket, flipped to his recent calls, and pressed the first entry. The line rang three times before connecting.

"Hi, honey."

"Hey, Mom."

"I thought you were going to call earlier. Are you okay?"

"I'm fine. How are things?"

"Have you been drinking?"

"No."

"It sounds like you've been drinking."

"Mom…"

Alex's mother sighed. "Things are fine. Weather hasn't been much to be excited about. I talked to Cheryl and Billy yesterday. They're doing good, looking forward to the boys being home over Christmas break."

"That's good."

"Grandma had a doctor's appointment on Tuesday. Thought she was dying. Turns out, it was acid reflux."

"Yeah, you mentioned it yesterday."

"Oh, right." She paused. "You sure everything's okay? Don't you have a meeting tonight?"

Alex cleared his throat. "Yeah, it just ended."

"How'd it go?"

Alex lowered his head and turned away from a couple strolling along the sidewalk. "It was good. Just another meeting, you know?"

"That's good."

The phone fell silent.

"Okay, I'll let you go. It's late."

"Sounds good. You'll call me tomorrow?"

"For sure."

"Okay. Love you."

"Love you too, Mom."

A pair of club girls, in dresses that appeared painted on, giggled as they walked past.

Alex waited for the call to disconnect and slipped his phone back in his pocket. He cut in front of the line at the bar and slapped the bouncer on his shoulder as he walked by, paying no regard to the complaints raised behind him. Pausing in the entryway, the sharp scent of sanitizer bloomed as he rubbed the gel over his hands. Alex maneuvered into the crowd, caring little for who, or how, he displaced the room full of revelers. At the bar, he reached between Taz and the flavor of the night for the fresh beer set out for him.

Through the music and loud talking, he heard shouting and the stomping feet of someone off balance. By instinct, his upper body rotated, and he struck out with his free hand. The drunk recoiled from the impact, tottered back, then folded to the floor. Alex held out his beer for Taz to take, then leaped forward to straddle the man.

"I said, last chance, you piece of shit."

Fists as tight as rocks smashed into the drunk's face. Again and again, until blood stained the open floor. The friend and others tried to intervene, but were easily shoved aside. Alex was only stopped when Taz charged him, like a bull would a red cape, and tackled him to the floor.

FIVE

Jacob shifted in bed and pulled the covers tight to his chin. Chilled air held a faint hint of car exhaust. He rolled over and eyed the room. A sliver of light came through the crack in the open door. The pillows on Mati's bed were askew, and the sheets tossed to one side.

Jacob walked to the motel room door. One of Mati's shoes held it out from the frame. Jacob pulled the door open and stepped onto the walkway.

Mati leaned against the railing with the hood of her sweater pushed back, watching stray stars moving in and out of view around high, thin clouds, and the halo around the moon. One socked foot rested on the other. Sam curled up on the ground to her left. When Jacob stood beside Mati, she looked to him from the corner of her eye.

Jacob tucked his hands in the pockets of his shorts. "Everything okay?"

Mati focused back on the night sky. "Yeah."

Jacob waited for more, but it did not come. He looked out to the parking lot, half filled with sleeping vehicles, and the darkness beyond. He nodded upward. "Looks like a full moon."

"It was. Yesterday."

"Oh. With everything else going on, I guess I didn't notice."

Mati altered her stance and pulled her hands into her sleeves. "I've always liked the moon. It's what my name means." She paused and chewed on her lower lip. "I feel connected, I guess. She's been through a lot, just like me. Survived meteors and asteroids. Forever slipping away because the earth isn't strong enough to hold on to her." She half-turned to Jacob and tucked a stray clutch of dark hair behind her ear. "In some ways, I want to be like the moon. Proudly display my scars, to show the beauty that violence can bring. I want to say to the world that no matter what I've been through, I'm here. If I'm still fighting to hold on, maybe you can, too."

"We could all use a little more of that. To know we're not alone. That maybe everything will be okay."

Mati pursed her lips and nodded.

Jacob stood back and crossed his arms high on his chest. "I'm going to head in."

Mati looked down at her hands. "Okay."

Jacob turned and pushed through the door, being careful not to move the shoe propped up at the bottom.

———

Jacob faced away from the window with his eyes closed tight, but the rising sun could not be unseen. Rolling to his back, he let out a long breath. Dryness in his mouth made it uncomfortable to swallow. The alarm clock beside him flashed red eights. He reached under the pillow for his watch and held it close to his face. Ticking hands showed seven forty-eight.

He squinted in the direction of Mati's bed. Slept-in sheets were pulled up over the pillows. Jacob sat up and stretched his arms. He reached again under the pillow to check for his wallet, then leaned over the other side of his bed to check for his bag. Moving to swing his legs down, he stopped at the click of the door. Mati walked into the room. "Morning. I took Sam for a walk. She's in the truck. We're ready to go when you are."

"Sounds good." Jacob gave a tired smile. "Give me ten minutes."

"Okay." She tossed the key onto the end of her bed and walked out the door.

———

Electronic bells chimed when Jacob opened the motel office door. Heavy condensation on the truck's windshield steamed under the crisp sky and rising sun. Mati leaned up against the side of the box and watched traffic speed past.

Jacob set a hand on the driver's door and pulled the keys from his coat pocket. "Ready?"

Mati stood forward. "Yup."

"You sure you still want to come along? Might be easier to head east from here."

"You trying to get rid of me?"

Jacob smiled. "No, of course not."

"I figure I've got a better chance of catching another ride down there. We'll see, I guess."

"All right, let's go then." Jacob sat behind the wheel and

reached across to unlock the passenger door. Mati took her seat and settled in. Jacob turned the ignition and the engine rattled to life. A couple quick blasts of fluid on the windshield cleared the view as seatbelts clicked in place. He shifted the truck into gear and turned out of the lot toward Highway 1.

———

The pair spoke little as the outskirts of Toronto enveloped them. Jacob drove on, in no particular hurry, and parked beside the storefront of a gas station before the Highway 401 turnoff. He shut the engine down and turned to Mati.

She watched out the side window. "I guess this is my stop."

"You sure you don't want some lunch?"

"I'm okay."

Mati got out of the truck and set the strap of her bag over her shoulder. She went to the back and dropped the tailgate. "Let's go." Sam jumped down to the pavement and turned to sit beside her. Jacob put his hands in his pockets and kicked at a rock on the asphalt. Mati looked up the road.

"Listen, I don't want this to get all weird." Jacob pulled out a small stack of folded bills from his pocket. "This should get you to Montréal."

"I—"

"I know, I know. You can take care of yourself. I get it. Take the money. Please."

Mati reached out, took the money, and slid it to the bottom of her bag. "Thanks, Jacob. For everything. For being a good guy." Mati clicked the tailgate closed. "Come on, Sam."

A few steps along, she looked back and raised her hand.

Jacob returned the gesture. Mati focused her attention on the pavement at her feet and walked away.

Jacob pumped gas and watched the path that led Mati away, though she was long gone. With the tank full, he headed south on the 404. The grumble in his stomach signaled a burger and a drink to go would not be a bad idea. He ate behind the wheel in silence. The distraction that Mati provided over the previous couple days became apparent. Jacob had not given much thought to his own situation, but the hope that everything might work out would soon be tested.

He took the 401 West to avoid Toronto proper. The 403 took him to Queen Elizabeth Way, and along the edge of Lake Ontario, before turning off north of Fort Erie. He worried he might get lost, but it all came back to him soon enough. He drove under the highway, then across Black Creek. Right onto the narrow two-lane road heading south and left around a sweeping bend. Asphalt transitioned to patchy gravel. At one point, he slowed the truck and checked his mirrors, thinking he had gone too far. That's when he saw it.

Faded and peeling paint on the sign was half-covered by an overgrown tree. Jacob kept his speed down as he turned up the drive and along the narrow, rutted road. Once the tree cover cleared, he was able to take everything in.

Eight single wide houses were positioned around a central greenspace. All had a parking pad that led to the front door. A couple had garages built behind. Jacob followed the road up and around before stopping at lot number six, one in from the south-west corner. Heavy curtains blocked windows covered in dust and framed with cobwebs. Weeds overran the patchy grass. The broken realty sign laid on the ground beside the front walk.

Jacob's grandparents spent most of their married life in

Hamilton. Gordon worked at a local steel mill. Delia stayed at home to raise five children, the youngest being Jacob's mother, Renae. After the children had grown and moved on to lives and families of their own, and as Gordon neared retirement, a private equity firm bought the mill. In the first round of restructuring, Gordon was packaged off. Left with an empty house, and a healthy pension to fall back on, Gordon and Delia decided a quiet place to retire would be just the ticket. And so, they became one of the first residents of Niagara Country Village.

Jacob stood in front of his truck with his arms crossed. Long forgotten memories came fresh to his mind. The shed out back, full of his grandfather's woodworking projects. The vegetable garden beside the house, and smaller flower gardens scattered around the property that his grandmother had doted over. He could hear the creak of the third porch step and smell fresh baking coming from the kitchen. Then, he remembered the time he tripped running up the driveway, skinning both knees and the palms of his hands. His grandmother gave him ice cream, with multi-colored sprinkles and chocolate sauce, for a whole week after.

Jacob jolted back to the present at the sound of someone clearing their throat behind him.

"Can I help you, young man?"

Jacob turned to see an older woman with short, dark hair, flecked with silver, framing her soft face. Through thick-framed glasses perched on the end of her nose, pale green eyes kept a close watch on him. With the sleeves of her floral print dress folded up to her elbows, she wiped her hands on a dish towel.

"I was just stopping to check out the house."

The woman squinted her eyes and pushed her glasses back up on her nose. "Jake? Is that you?"

Jacob cocked his head.

The woman turned behind her. "Penny, look, it's Jake. *Quick, come see.*"

Shielding her eyes with one hand, another woman descended the porch steps from the neighboring house with her lips held in a tight line. She showcased her slim figure in a stylish blouse, fitted pants, and a pair of plush, burgundy slippers. Her artificial chestnut hair was tied in a twist behind her head. Numerous bangles and bracelets chimed together as she brought her free hand up to cover her open mouth.

"You remember little Jake, don't you?"

Penny lowered her hand and gave a wry smile. "Well, he isn't so little anymore, is he?"

"Oh, Penny…"

Jacob shuffled his feet and blushed as recognition dawned. "Hi, Gwen. Hi, Penny."

Jacob thought back to his second-to-last summer with his grandparents, the year Penny first came to the community. She was the topic of many conversations at the time. Rumor was her fourth marriage had come to an end, so she decided to be done with commitment and moved in with her sister, Gwen.

"My lord, it's been years. How have you been? Where have you been all this time?"

"I've been okay, I guess. I moved down south a couple years after Dad passed, and Mom left for Peru. The only time I've been back was for, well, you know. Sorry I didn't have a chance to catch up with you guys then."

Gwen waved her hand and turned back toward her house. "Oh, don't worry about that, dear. Come on over to our place, you can fill us in. Water is on for a pot of tea, and there are cookies in the oven. You're just in time."

"Thank you, that sounds good. And it's Jacob now, if that's okay."

"Of course, it's okay. It's your name, isn't it? Come on, then."

Gwen ushered Jacob into the kitchen and laid out ample quantities of hot tea and fresh oatmeal raisin cookies. Jacob did his best to catch them up on the last ten years. Luckily, the cookies and tea outlasted his tale.

"So, what's going on around here?" Jacob looked to the front window. "Honestly, it doesn't look like much has changed."

"Well, that's a bit of a story, now isn't it?"

"Gwendolyn Carrol, please don't bore the boy…"

"Oh, fine, the short version then. You know, this all used to be farmland. Most things were, if you go back far enough, I guess. So, old man Benson passed in the mid-eighties. The kids ended up selling off most of the land, to pay debts I hear, and then made plans to develop what was left. They set up the eight houses that are here, and were ready to go ahead with more, before everything went off the tracks." Gwen smiled wide, and nudged Penny with her elbow.

"Oh, Gwen…"

"So, it turns out, there was a rail line near here around a hundred years ago." Gwen put her hands flat on the table and leaned forward. "Off the tracks. Get it?" She rested back in her chair. "Anyway, someone found chemicals in the ground, and the enviro-hippies put an end to the whole thing, tout suite."

"Gwen, *please*."

"Well, it's true, isn't it? Nobody wanted to pay the bill, or couldn't afford to, as I might have mentioned. One of the kids had the bright idea of turning it all back into farmland and put an end to the whole issue, but then the hippies said no. It's the habitat of a rare salamander or some such nonsense. The family started fighting amongst themselves, and now it's all tied up with the lawyers. Scum of the earth, they are. Who knows what's going to happen now?"

"It's all such a shame, really." Penny motioned with one hand. "Look at your grandparent's place, absolutely nothing wrong with it, but we haven't seen anyone come to have a look in months. Why would someone risk it, knowing we might all be kicked out by spring?"

"It really is terrible, but enough about that. What are your plans, dear? Now that you're back, where are you going to stay?"

Jacob pushed the handle of his mug back and forth on the table. "Honestly? I don't really know."

"You mean you came all this way and don't have a place to stay?"

"No. I guess not."

"Well, we'll fix that." Gwen stood and shuffled into the next room.

Jacob and Penny sat at the table. Penny tapped the side of her mug with her French manicure. Jacob fidgeted in his chair and stared at his hands. Gwen talked away in the next room, far enough out that the details muddled. She fell silent and came back into the kitchen, then stretched her arm out to Jacob with an old cordless phone in her hand. "Jacob, it's your Aunt Tanya. She wants to talk to you."

———

"Thanks, Tanya. This really means a lot to me."

"I'm glad to help. Be sure to call if you need anything, anything at all."

"I will. Thanks again."

"Okay, talk to you soon, Jacob."

"Bye."

Jacob pressed the disconnect button and handed the phone back to Gwen. "Thank you."

"Did you two get everything figured out, dear?"

"Yeah, I think we did."

"Excellent news."

"I hope so. I mean, I don't think I've talked to her that much in the last twenty years."

Gwen looked to her watch. "Well, you were on the phone almost an hour."

"Yeah, sorry."

"No need to be sorry, dear. What did you two decide, then?"

"Well, she said it's okay for me to stay at the house, as long as I can fix a few things up that are out of place. She's going to make a few calls to get the power and phone set up and talk to a friend about a job for me. Something to start off with, at least."

Penny smiled. "That sounds about perfect."

Gwen pushed back from the table. "Well, why don't we get you set up here for the night? First thing tomorrow, we can open up the house and start tidying up for your stay."

Jacob smiled. "That would be great. Thank you."

SIX

Jacob double-checked his fly, then wandered into the living room.

"Good morning, dear."

"Morning."

"How'd you sleep?"

"Good, thanks."

"Good. Grab a coffee and have a seat. Breakfast is almost ready."

Jacob filled a mug and sat on the far side of the table. He tensed at the sensation of pressure on his leg, then came a purr and the flick of a tail. The mottled long-haired cat looked up at Jacob, but with no sign of an offered treat, it sauntered off to the living room and curled up on the love seat.

A plate overflowing with bacon, one piled high with slices of fried potatoes, and a bowl of scrambled eggs with a large spoon sticking out, sat in the center of the table. Gwen placed a smaller bowl of diced fruit and a stack of buttered toast next to them.

Penny came into the kitchen with her hair and makeup

done, dressed in an outfit that gave the impression she had an important meeting planned. She sat at the table with her back straight. "Good morning. How was your sleep?"

"Morning, Penny." Jacob rubbed at his eye. "Actually, I don't think I've slept that well in a long time."

"Good to hear."

Gwen placed a mug of coffee in front of Penny. "All right, everyone dish up."

Jacob waited until Penny and Gwen had taken their share before filling his own plate.

"Oh, Gwen, I saw Harold when I was out for my walk. He wondered about Jacob's truck in front of the Winthrop's place. I filled him in about what's going on."

"Harold, is he…" Jacob squinted and pointed in the direction of the road in.

"He is, and I guess since you're staying, we'd better catch you up on who the neighbors are."

Jacob nodded with a thin smile. "Guess so."

Gwen sat forward in her chair. "Well, Harold lives on the end here. He's been with us for, oh, eleven or twelve years now."

Penny took a sip from her coffee and set it back on the table. "Poor dear is on his own. His wife Martha passed almost two years ago. You might remember her. Lovely woman. The family comes to visit during the summer and sometimes at Christmas. Mostly, he goes to them. His first great-grandbaby was born last year. He's pretty self-sufficient, but when he needs it, we all help out."

"He really is doing well, all things considered. Such a sweetheart too, I think you'll like him."

"He fought in Vietnam. Came to Canada in ninety or ninety-one, I think. He doesn't talk about it much, which is understandable, but he keeps both flags on his front porch. A little piece of home, I suppose."

"Next to you are Nicolas and Malena. 'Fraid I don't know a whole lot about them as they tend to keep to themselves. They're some sort of Spanish. I think their place was a summer house, then around twenty-ten, they moved here full time. Never seen any kids, and they rarely have any visitors."

"I'm sure they're lovely people, but what we're saying is, you probably won't see too much of them."

"Now, one house over is a different situation."

"Oh, Lord, is it ever..."

"You'd probably remember Leroy and Marilyn, they lived there for a lot of years. After they won the lottery and moved to port-of-something-or-other—"

"It's Puerto Vallarta, Gwen. I keep telling you..."

"I know, I know. Anyway, they left the house to their boys. It wasn't bad with just Clint and Erica, and their two little ones, Allena and Parker. Then, Davie moved in..."

"He lives in a camper in the backyard."

"And then poor Erica got pregnant again. With little Hayden, there's five of them in that small house."

"She's got a heart of gold, that one."

"She is wonderful. I have no idea how she got wrapped up with that group of white trash."

"Easy now, Gwen..."

"For the love of everything, they use a kiddie pool to hold their beer in the summer, and there's a Camaro on the front lawn. *An actual Camaro.*"

Penny waved the thought away and leaned in toward Jacob. "It's not as bad as Gwen makes it out to be. They are a little obnoxious sometimes, but they're easy enough to get along with. The kids don't get into too much trouble either..."

"Amazingly enough."

"Oh, Gwen…"

"Anyway, enough about them. You'll figure it out soon enough on your own, I'm sure. Back in the other corner is Francois and Rosana Fournier. They'll have been here three years come spring. Francois said they wanted to get away from some family issues they were having in Québec City."

"If you use such an innocent term to describe stealing your cousin's wife…"

"We don't know that for sure, but we've heard some things, you know? Francois says he used to work with Rosana way back. They met again when they were both on vacation in Vancouver and ended up spending most of their time there together…"

Penny raised her eyebrows. "Some very quality time, I'm sure."

"They haven't really been apart since. Francois owns a business that exports plastic and aluminum for recycling, so the short distance to the border and shipping routes is good for him, I guess."

"It's good for Rosana's shopping habit, too."

"She really is something else. So beautiful, could have been a model, that one."

"And she knows it, doesn't she?"

"Don't get me wrong, Francois is nice and all, very funny too, but I never did understand those two together. I'm sure they're very happy, but they seem so different. Rosana's a fair bit younger than he is."

Penny raised an eyebrow. "She's not as young as she dresses, though…"

"She pushes it sometimes, I'll give you that. One of her

favorite things is to have a smoke out on the front porch in nothing but her nightgown.”

"She's a hoor, is what she is."

Gwen waved her away. "Penny, you're just jealous."

Penny wrapped both hands around her mug and turned her nose up.

The phone rang, and they all looked up to its spot on the kitchen wall.

"Now, who would be calling at this time of day?" Gwen stood and picked the handset up from its cradle. "Hello?"

She stood with her free hand supporting her elbow, and she held one eye half-shut.

"I'm sorry, but I can't understand a single thing you're saying. We only speak English here." Gwen squeezed down on the end button with her thumb, then set the handset back on the wall. Jacob kept his eyes on the table and pushed around a few scraps of scrambled egg on his plate.

"Anyway." Gwen sat back in her chair. "The house next to Francois and Rosana, that's where a couple named Dan and Terri used to live. Odd pair those two. Hadn't been here more than two years, before one day, they just up and left in the middle of the night."

"Nobody knows what happened, and there hasn't been anyone around since they went away."

"Very strange indeed, but that's all there is to say about that, really. Now, the first house, on the other side in, belongs to George and Darina Miller. They've been here a long time. George is nice. He puts a lot of work into their place and does all of it himself, including the garage out back."

"He's certainly particular, that one. Likes things just so."

Jacob shifted in his seat. "Yeah, I seem to remember him shouting at me once when I followed one of Gwen's cats through his yard. Said I was going to wreck his lawn or something."

"He's not all bad. His wife on the other hand…" Gwen arched her eyebrows and got up to grab the coffee pot.

"Easy now."

Gwen pursed her lips and looked at Penny from the corner of her eye as she refilled their mugs. "That woman is something else. Always smiles and has pleasant things to say in front of your face, but that changes when you turn your back."

Penny's eyes went wide. She turned away from Gwen and spoke half-under her breath. "Not like anyone else we know."

If Gwen noticed, she did not show it. "How long has it been since you saw their kids come to visit, Penny?"

"I don't know. It's been a while."

"A long while. I know she keeps poor George on a short leash. I've heard her screaming at him, too. You can hear it right through the walls. I wouldn't be surprised if it gets worse than that sometimes."

Penny stared at her coffee and said nothing.

"That just leaves the Bensons, I guess. See, old man Benson—"

"He had a name, Gwen."

Gwen eyed Penny. "Ray was born on the main property out across the road. I'm sure if he had his way, he would've died on it too. He married Deborah in the pasture out back. They raised their kids in the same house he grew up in. The only thing more important to him than that farm was his family. Times change though, sometimes we need to learn to change with them. Or leave it to our kids once we kick the bucket."

"Oh, for heaven's sake, Gwen."

"I'm just saying what's true, Penny, and you know it. After old man…after Ray passed on, Andrew and his wife Cassandra moved back home to help his mom keep the place moving. Being the oldest and the only son, that's what you get, I suppose. He wanted to do the right thing, but he was also busy with his small engine repair business, mostly boats and such. I guess I already told you how all of that worked out. His sister Patricia and her husband Nathan moved to the States shortly after they were married, so they weren't going to be much help anyway. Andrew and Cassie had two boys, the last moved out a couple years back. Now, it's just the two of them, and Deborah of course, but she mostly just stays around the house these days."

"So sad. She's such a wonderful lady."

Gwen set her fork and knife on her plate and moved her mug toward the center of the table. "I guess that gets you all caught up. That's the neighborhood."

Penny leaned forward over her coffee. "So, what do you have planned for your day, Jacob?"

"I'm not sure. There's a lot to choose from. I've got to get the house cleaned up, then grab some groceries and such. Should get to the bank and get an account set up, but there's time. I was hoping to make a call before I head out. I've got a friend in Toronto I haven't talked to in a while. Maybe do some laundry. Tomorrow, I'm going to go meet with a friend of Aunt Tanya's. He's looking for framers."

"Sounds like a real good start."

"Yeah, I hope so."

Gwen scooped a heaping spoonful of scrambled eggs on to Jacob's plate. "Eat up then. It's going to be a busy day."

SEVEN

Taz walked through the glass-paned door but reached back to hold it open. He glanced at the words 'criminal court' carved in the stonework above it. Alex followed out onto the sidewalk, dark sunglasses covering his bloodshot eyes and the edges of a bruise on his cheek. They turned to head west on East 161st. A police officer dashed forward to catch the door before it closed, but stopped to eye the pair.

"Another eventful night out, hey Becker?"

Alex let out a breath and looked along the street.

Taz shook his head. "Mind your own, Frankie."

The officer pointed a finger. "Hey, that's Officer Rivera to you, jackass." He wiped at his nose. "Have a good one, Becker. Say hi to your mommy for me."

Alex spun and, in two steps, stood nose-to-nose with Rivera. Taz caught him fast and held his arms. "Whoa, whoa. Let the cell cool down, at least."

Alex locked eyes with Rivera. His face glowed with color.

Rivera sneered. "Come on, tough guy. You ain't half as big as you need to be."

Taz eased Alex back. "Alex, let's go."

Alex wrinkled his nose and turned away.

"Yeah, that's what I thought."

Alex did not look back. "Fuck you, Rivera."

Taz sighed.

Rivera pushed the door wide open. "Good job keeping your boyfriend under control, Vincent."

Taz glanced back before walking on. "Fuck you, Officer Rivera."

Rivera pulled up on his belt and looked around to see who might have noticed, then walked into the courthouse.

Taz stayed a step behind Alex as he stormed down the sidewalk. "You hungry?"

Alex grunted a reply.

"Good. Me too. And guess who's paying? I'll give you a hint, it's the guy who didn't just drain his bank account to bail his best friend out."

Alex slowed his pace and rested against the concrete wall. His sunglasses focused on the ground. "You know I appreciate it."

"I know, man. Just giving you the gears."

Alex shrugged.

"When's your court date?"

"I don't know, couple weeks."

"You know you got lucky, right? This one could'a been a felony."

Alex ignored the question.

Taz pushed out a breath and scratched his forehead. "What do you think you want to do?"

"I don't know. Breakfast sounds good."

"Naw, I mean, bigger picture?"

"Oh." Alex watched people walking each way along the

sidewalk. "Think maybe it's time for a road trip, get away for a bit."

Taz nodded. "Sounds like a plan." He stepped away from the wall and into the pedestrian flow. "But first, *we eat.*"

EIGHT

Jacob surveyed each room, opening windows as he went to release the stale air. The house looked like a hungry bear had rummaged through it. The sight of it disheartened him. Sad, what the remains of a life could be reduced to, how people could treat what was left behind, even if those people were your family.

With a bucket of hot, soapy water in hand, Jacob worked his way around the kitchen, wiping counters and the interior of the fridge as it cooled. In the living room, an ancient upright vacuum worked across the rose hued carpet. He wondered if it was doing much good. Next, he mopped the linoleum floors in the kitchen, dining area, and bathroom. While the floors dried, he walked to the top of the hall and stared at his grandparent's bedroom door shut tight at the end. Jacob thought it over for a moment, then turned toward the guest room. He stood in the doorway with his arms spread, and his hands high on the molding.

In one corner, a bare mattress on a basic frame. Boxes, stacked awkwardly on top of each other, had piles of clothes and bunched up blankets scattered around them. The plain walls were void of any sort of decoration.

Jacob let out a deep breath and entered the room. He pulled everything out of the closet, sorted boxes, packed a few more, then stacked them back inside. Extra wool blankets were folded and set on the top shelf, but he kept a flower-patterned comforter by the door. With the floor clear, Jacob pulled the bed from the wall to the middle of the room and placed the nightstand on the right-hand side. After he clipped the shade back onto the deco lamp, he set it on the nightstand and plugged it into the wall. Last, he fanned out the comforter and draped it over the bed.

Jacob stood back, and a smile crept across his face. It had been a long time since he used a single bed, but it would do.

He paused in front of his grandparent's bedroom door with a laundry basket balanced on his left hip. Armed with a set of clean sheets, a bottle of glass cleaner, and a roll of paper towel, he let out a slow breath and pushed the door open.

Sun-bleached linen curtains hung loose across the window. A beam of sunshine highlighted specs of dust floating through the air. Jacob set the laundry basket down on a corner of the bed and sat beside it. Empty picture frames littered the top of the dresser. Decorative plates created a pattern on the wall.

It smelled the same as he remembered. It brought to mind the day he got the phone call. How deflated he felt, the physical pain that ran in waves through his body.

Jacob's grandparents were on their way home after Delia's regular appointment at the hairdresser. It was warm for the time of year, and not a cloud in the sky. As if that could have changed anything. A drunk driver, doing nearly twice the limit, crossed into their lane. The police said they died instantly. Jacob hoped it was true, because sometimes an instant can last forever.

He was on the road, of course, south of Minneapolis. He got home as fast as he could and took the next available flight to Hamilton. Charlotte's uncle had another run scheduled for him, so Jacob left right after the funeral. Duncan said it was important, no one else was available to take it for him. Jacob knew he should have fought harder, but for whatever reason, he did not. It was good to catch up with his family and he was thankful for the time he got. Everyone came, except his mother. He heard she could not get a flight in time.

The little support that Jacob had disappeared after he was back across the border. The feeling of aloneness left him empty, so he did what he always did in those situations and threw himself into his work. At home, he would put on a brave face, spending most of his time reading or working on his truck. He tried to be the person that Charlotte and her friends expected him to be. Though it had only been days, it all seemed like a lifetime ago.

Jacob sniffed and wiped at the corners of his eyes. He stood and moved the laundry basket to the floor, stripped the bed, and started a dirty laundry pile beside the open bedroom door. Any clothes scattered across the floor were tossed onto the growing pile. He straightened up anything hanging in the closet, and he tidied the tops of the nightstands and the dresser along the window wall. Soon after, the curtains dropped down to the dirty laundry pile. It took two passes with the cleaner and towels to get the window glass clear. Jacob laid out fresh sheets on the bed and even fluffed the pillows, but afterward, felt silly for doing so. He pushed a short stack of boxes into the closet and paused to look around the room. Things were looking good, but he made a mental note to bring the vacuum in later.

The first signs of dusk filled the now clean windows. After glancing at his watch, Jacob pushed the overflowing laundry basket into the hall and closed the door behind him. It had been a productive day, but it was time to call it quits. Gwen had invited him over for dinner, and he did not want to be late.

NINE

Mati sat on the curb outside a row of businesses not yet open for the day. She watched across the parking lot while her phone dialed out.

"Hello?"

"Dad? It's Mati."

Mati heard echoing footsteps and a door close. "Hello, Matisa. How did you…it's been a while. How have you been?"

"I don't know. Okay." Mati sniffed. "I'm in Kingston."

"Kingston? What are you doing in Kingston?"

"I thought I would come out for a visit. I…I've been looking into school and—"

"School?"

"Yeah. I've been applying for scholarships."

"Matisa," her father sighed. "You should have called. Before now, I mean."

"Sorry, I just needed to get out. I didn't really have a plan."

"How…how's your mother doing?"

"Not sure." Mati pressed her shoulder to hold the cell phone against her ear and crossed her arms. "Haven't seen her in weeks."

"Why? What's going on?"

"Nothing good."

"I'm sorry." The line fell silent. "Listen, there are some things you need to know."

"Okay." Mati checked behind her and wiped at a tear on her cheek.

"Your mother and I were very young when we got together. I'm sure I don't need to explain, but we both made mistakes. I wish…I wish I could have been there for you. I do. It just didn't work out that way."

Mati bowed her head and picked at a loose thread on the cuff of her sleeve. "Yeah."

"I forget sometimes that you're, well, you're a grown woman. I haven't been good about keeping in touch. That's my fault, not yours. It's just something I'm not good at. There's a lot you don't know. So much has changed, Matisa. I have a family." He exhaled into the phone. "You have a sister. She just turned eleven."

"A sister." Mati stared off at nothing in particular.

"Like I said, things are different. I didn't think I would get married again. Not ever. But I met Emma, and all that changed. I don't want you to think that you or your mother…I mean that you could—"

"It's okay, I get it."

"No, really. I know I could have done better. Maybe, sometimes, I was just ashamed of leaving the way I did. I couldn't face you."

Mati's voice was faint. "I would have taken a not perfect dad over no dad at all."

"I'm sorry. I guess I didn't think that way at the time."

They were quiet as Mati worked up the courage to ask her next question. "Do you think maybe things can change?"

"I mean, we've just got a little place. It's perfect for the three of us, but…"

"I won't get in the way, I promise. I just need a place to crash until—"

"Matisa, I don't know."

"Please, Dad. I need you to come pick me up."

Dead air on the line did nothing to slow the pace of her heart.

"I'm sorry, Matisa. I can't."

The connection ended.

"Dad?"

Mati watched the screen of her phone as it went dark. She slipped it into her pocket, then leaned forward, head in her hands, and shook as the tears flowed.

TEN

Jacob slowed and pulled to the right shoulder as Penny's Cadillac descended the driveway. He rolled down his window and rested an elbow on the door. "Hey, guys."

Gwen called from the passenger seat. "Hello, dear. Seems that didn't take long, how'd your meeting go?"

"Not long at all. I start on Monday."

"Excellent news."

Jacob shrugged. "I think so. Where are you off to?"

"The grocery store. Haven't you heard? The storm of the century is coming."

Gwen leaned over Penny's lap. "They say it's the polar vortex. New York State has basically been shut down. *The end of the world is coming our way.*"

"Wow, guess I need to pay better attention to the forecast."

"Do you need us to pick anything up for you?"

Jacob raked his fingertips through the short beard on his chin. "No, I should be good."

"Okay, see you in a bit, then."

Gwen waved as Penny pressed down on the accelerator of

the Coupe Deville. In seconds, they drove around the bend and out of sight.

Jacob parked and grabbed his bag from the passenger seat. He shuffled past the realty sign propped against the house and climbed the porch steps to unlock the front door. Inside, he dropped his bag beside the boot mat and draped his coat over one of the chairs at the kitchen table. Making his way into the living room, he flopped down on the old recliner, then pulled out the remote from between the cushion and the arm. Local news rang into the room, and Jacob relaxed into his spot. He watched for a few minutes before flipping channels.

"The US National Weather Service is warning of a super storm forming over New York State that will soon envelop the entire east coast…"

Click.

"As you can see, Kelly, the roads are absolutely jam packed with commuters trying to get home before mandatory closures come in to effect at seven o'clock tonight…"

Click.

"…spokesperson says that over five thousand flights have been canceled in New York alone…"

Click.

"…shelves are nearing empty as people stock up on water and canned goods…"

Click.

The screen went dark, and Jacob dropped the remote beside him. He ran a hand over his head and looked toward the kitchen.

After sorting through all the drawers and cupboards, he set his bounty out on the table. Packs of matches sat next to a group of half-burned Christmas candles, along with a flashlight and extra batteries, for good measure. As far as survival kits went, it lacked quite a bit, but it would have to do. Jacob grabbed a glass from beside the sink and filled it from the tap. Drinking it down, he tugged the kitchen curtains open. Dark clouds, shaped like anvils, filled the sky to the south. Jacob glanced over to a picture of his grandparents hanging on the wall. A saying his grandfather was fond of came to him then—that's a bad one coming, I can feel it in my bones.

ELEVEN

Alex zipped his coat as the door to the restaurant jangled closed behind him. Patchy slush lined the street. Falling snow started sticking to the sidewalk. As the sun set, the heaviness in the sky showed no sign of easing.

Taz crushed his cigarette against the side of the building, then flicked the butt to be lost among the falling flakes. "Christ, about time. Thought you fell in."

"Had to wash my hands."

"Did you sing 'Happy Birthday' thirty fucking times?"

Alex shoved his hands into his pockets and pushed out a breath.

"Right. I'd like to get moving before this bullshit gets any worse."

Alex nodded, but focused south along the freeway. A string of headlights, back to back, approached at speed. Howling engines filled the air as the line of SUVs, with a light armored vehicle bringing up the rear, advanced and flashed past. All black. No markings. As the taillights faded, the snow resumed its regular pattern. Taz looked to Alex. Alex watched the empty road.

"What d'ya think that was all about?"

"Not sure."

"I suppose you're gonna wanna figure it out."

Alex did not answer. Instead, he made his way toward the parking lot. Taz pulled a ring of keys from his pocket and spun them on his finger. "You remember you don't do that stuff anymore, right?"

Alex stalked away.

"Okay. Let's go then."

TWELVE

A rusted-out minivan, with its exhaust rattling and its remaining hubcap moments from letting go, moved fast on Highway 403 heading west, swerving back and forth between the lanes with little regard for other vehicles on the road. Mati crouched in the back with Sam. She could barely think over the droning beat coming from the oversized speaker in the opposite corner. Sam huddled close to her side, shaking. Taking the ride had been a mistake, but with the temperature dropping and the snow growing heavier, it seemed like the best option at the time.

The driver and his girlfriend sat up front. He leaned back in his seat with one hand resting over the top of the wheel. She flipped her shoulder length blue hair around to the beat. The third wheel, Mati assumed the driver's friend, stretched out across the middle seat, his long sandy mane matted into dreads. A couple of times, he found motivation to draw shapes in the condensation on the sliding door window, but otherwise stayed slumped over, sleeping, or too high to move.

Mati checked her phone. No notifications. She checked

the time, thinking she misread the numbers. It had only been twenty minutes. With the phone back in her pocket, she rose to glance out the window, then turned toward the front and made eye contact with the driver in the rear-view mirror. Holding her gaze, he lowered the volume on the stereo. He tilted his head to the side and shouted, "You all right back there?"

Mati bent forward on the middle seat. "Yeah."

The girlfriend spun around. Thick eyeliner highlighted her crisp, hazel eyes. A thin chrome hoop split the deep maroon smudged over her lower lip. "You want a beer?"

"No, I'm okay."

The girlfriend reached down to a battered to-go cup perched in between the front seats. She held up a joint, almost burned down to the crutch. Mati shook her head. The girlfriend shrugged and took a hit. The friend in the middle seat sat bolt upright. He fanned his extended fingers toward the girlfriend. After she passed him the joint, the friend rested it between his dry lips and pulled long and hard. He tilted his head back and exhaled slowly. Mati covered her nose and mouth with the ratty sleeve of her sweater.

The friend stretched his arms out over the back of the seat, what remained of the joint pinched between his thumb and forefinger. Dense smoke faded as it died out, and he dropped it to the floor of the van. "Man, I'm so fucked up right now." Hollow laughter, like the low churning of an engine failing to start, echoed in the small space.

The driver turned back. "Dude, did you seriously finish that off already?"

"Hey man, not my fault if you missed out."

"You're such a dick, Jessie."

"Calm down, Brit's got more."

The girlfriend looked over the back of her seat. "What are you talking about? I gave everything to you at the club."

"No way, didn't happen."

"Dude, I gave it to you when I went dancing."

The friend slapped an open palm against his forehead. A warped smile formed on his lips. "Oh shit, I left it with Tamela."

"*Fuck, man.* Why the hell do we keep bringing you along?"

"Hey, hey, hey, listen. I know a guy, right? He owes me."

"Probably the other way around…"

"Shut it. Listen, he's got some good shit too."

"You'd better not be wasting our time, Jessie."

"I'm not. *I swear.*"

"Fine. Where the hell are we going?"

Jessie leaned forward, hands grabbing onto the two front seats. "He's in Dundas. I promise, it's good, man."

Mati sat up. "Hey, I thought you were heading up to Barrie."

The driver cut the van to an off-ramp. "Change of plans."

"Can you let me out?"

"We're in the middle of fucking nowhere. Chill out. We'll get you there. If I'm late for work one more time, I'm fucked."

Mati sat with her back against the middle seat and hugged her knees to her chest. Sam shifted over and nudged her hand with her nose. Mati wiped away the tears tracking down her cheek, then scratched at Sam's ear. "It's okay. We'll be okay."

THIRTEEN

"We need to get closer."

Taz screwed up his face and looked away from the flashing lights and barricades. "What the hell is your damage?"

"You know what my damage is."

Taz shook his head. "Sometimes I wonder."

The pair looked on as black uniforms with assault rifles mixed in with the State Police. They reminded Alex of an anthill. At first glance, disorganized and chaotic, until you looked closer. Entire stretches of road along Lake Erie were blocked off. Concrete partitions capped each street facing the waterfront.

"What do you think they're getting ready for?"

"Not sure. That's why we need to get closer."

Taz shut the engine down and pulled the key from the tumbler. "All right. Let's go for a walk then."

Snow swirled around them. Taz followed Alex as he circled behind the building they had parked beside. Advancing toward the trooper manning the blockade, Alex removed his gloves, stuck them in his pocket, and tucked his mask under the collar of his jacket.

The trooper looped his thumbs in his belt and spread his feet wide. Alex stopped a few feet away, his hands at his sides, and motioned his chin across the barricade. "Looks serious."

The trooper remained stoic. "We've got everything under control. How did you guys get in here?"

Alex threw a thumb over his shoulder. "Swung around to see what's goin' on and got turned the wrong way. Came down the alley over there."

"You really shouldn't be here."

Alex gave a crooked smile. "I was just thinkin', I haven't seen this many boots on the ground since that whack job with the truck a couple years back."

The trooper cocked an eyebrow and looked Alex up and down. "You were there for Manhattan?"

"Second week on the job. I requested a transfer to counter-terrorism right after."

"Nice." The trooper lifted one hand over his shoulder. "Could probably use your help here."

"Yeah?"

The trooper looked both ways behind him. "To be honest, I got no clue what it is we're doin' here. Word came down from on high to assist, so here we are. Told it was above our paygrade."

"Shut up and do what you're told?"

The trooper shook his head. "You know it."

"All too well." Alex looked up. "This bullshit sure doesn't help."

"Damn right, it doesn't. Thing is, I heard a rumor," the trooper leaned forward. "all this ain't natural."

"Not natural how?"

"Like, it's man made."

"So, we can control the weather now?"

"Government can, apparently. Then again, the guy I heard it from has a blog about little green men from outer space."

"Fair enough." Alex glanced back to Taz. "We're gonna have a quick look around, if that's okay. Won't get in your way."

"You're good. Just keep your distance from the black suits. They don't have much in the way of a sense of humor."

"Will do. Stay safe."

The trooper nodded and turned away.

Taz fell in behind Alex. "Did you get what you need?"

"Don't know."

"Sure would be nice to get out of this and warm up."

"Soon."

Alex walked away from the barricade, down the length of the building, and past the mouth of a narrow alley. Busy eyes darted across surrounding rooftops and along both sides of the street. Taz nearly ran into him when he came to a sudden stop. Alex shielded his eyes against the snow and looked back. Taz tucked close to a wall and waited. Retracing his steps, Alex turned left up an alley. Taz snuck a look to the trooper before following him. "This doesn't look like soon to me."

Near the end of the alley, Alex hauled down a metal ladder, then squeezed up the cage surrounding it to the top of the building. He swung his legs up and over, then disappeared from sight.

Taz focused upward. "Shit." He hung his head, sighed deep, and pulled himself up the ladder.

Alex crouched at the front of the building. He adjusted his

mask over his nose, then pulled on his gloves. Taz stood a few steps behind with his hands in his pockets.

Howling sirens blared from the east. Below, the uniforms snapped to attention. Alex leaned over the building to his right. The trooper they left moments before stepped away from the barricade and pulled his service revolver. He shouted at someone to stop, and without hesitation, pulled the trigger three times. As the flashes faded, a white panel van roared into view. It bucked as it took the trooper under its wheels and plowed through a gap in the concrete barriers. Broken plastic and scraps of sheered bodywork showered down onto the trooper's fractured body. The van slid and stopped at an angle in the road, steam billowing from its broken grill. Shattered glass rimmed the back window. One front wheel twisted at an odd angle. A loose belt squealed as the engine revved, the back end kicked out, and the van accelerated north.

Taz stepped away and looked to the top of the ladder. "Maybe…maybe we should get outta here."

State Police cruisers flooded the road and surrounded the van. It stalled after an attempt to break away. Black uniforms melted out of the shadows. Shouting, at first, then the night erupted with sound and color. The van rocked with a thousand violent impacts. The staccato eased for a heartbeat, then the van exploded.

A fireball shot into the air. It flashed and expanded in a wide percussive ring. At the same time, an additional round shot higher into the sky. It expanded to an even wider ring and propelled a third and final round into the clouds.

Alex shielded his head with his arm as pressure from the blast pushed over him. Fire and debris screamed overhead and battered the building. Windows along the block shattered in a crashing symphony. A dull thud next to him made him turn.

Taz laid crumpled on the roof. Alex reached out and pulled him flat on his back. Deep red stains spread across the shredded fabric over Taz's chest. A gash ran from his cheek to his eye, the ragged edge of a shard of metal protruding from his temple. Alex pressed two fingers against Taz's throat. "Taz? Come on, man."

Taz's body shuddered. He exhaled a wet breath that flecked his lips with blood.

Alex pulled his hand away once he was sure the pulse beneath was gone for good, then sat back and watched snow settle on his friend's cooling skin.

Light flickered around him, dancing with the growing fires. A dark cloud drifted over the city. Even through his mask, the air felt bitter. Hearing movement, Alex peered over the roof's edge. Everything inside the blast radius had turned to ash, charred and uneven. Outside the radius, bodies, or parts of them, littered the ground. A soldier in black, helmet missing, and hair matted to his head with blood, dragged himself to one of his fallen comrades. He dug under the slumped form and pulled out a radio receiver on a coiled cord. The soldier brought it to his mouth, said a few words, paused, then spoke again. A hasty response crackled. The soldier slumped and was still.

Alex backed away from the edge of the building. Near the middle, he stood and froze. The air snapped, taking all light with it. Alex turned one way and the other, but the shroud of darkness expanded for miles. He instinctively closed his eyes to allow them to adjust. When he opened them, he saw well enough to make his way down the ladder to the alley. With feet on the ground, he bolted away from the building to find the rental.

FOURTEEN

Jacob stared at the shadows across the wall, the bed covers tucked to his chin. Memories of a dream pulled at him, but the details faded with each breath. The air hung still and quiet. More than that, it lacked sound.

He reached out for the lamp and flipped the switch. Nothing. He toggled it back and forth with no different result. The alarm clock sat dark on the nightstand. Jacob pushed the sheets down, but quickly clawed them back over his naked body. "*Jesus.*"

Goosebumps flooded his skin against the chilled air. A flashback of the few times he went camping as a kid rushed to mind. Distant cold mornings in an orange canvas tent. Having to stash his clothes at the bottom of his sleeping bag to keep them warm.

He leaned over the edge of the bed, right arm shooting out to search the floor for his clothes. He pulled them under the covers and held them close to his body. "Holy sh-sh-sh…"

After the chill subsided, Jacob wrestled to dress under the blankets. Sock feet dropped to the carpet and shuffled to the bedroom door. With one arm held out in front of him, he slid the other along the unlit wall and navigated toward the kitchen.

He parted the curtains over the sink. Outside, he saw a different scene than when he closed his eyes a few hours earlier. Thick layers of white covered the landscape. Snow continued to fall in large, irregular clumps. Faint voices sounded through the window glass. Jacob lifted his jacket from the kitchen chair, zipped it to the top, put on his boots, and pushed through the front door.

A small group gathered in the central greenspace. Gwen and Penny had their backs to Jacob as he plowed his way through the snow to join them. The pair each wore sweaters over their house coats. Penny had a coarse knit hat covering down to her ears.

"Jacob," Gwen waved him on as he neared, "can you believe this?"

Jacob looked up. "This storm is no joke."

"I've never seen anything like it."

A man to their right, with waves of dirty blonde hair sticking out from the hood of his puffy camo jacket, stepped toward Jacob. "Hey, you must be the grandson." His extended hand showed fingernails stained with dirt and grease. "Clint." Clint's work boots were untied, and the tongues flopped forward. He had his free hand held low to his side, with a lit cigarette between his fingers.

Jacob shook his hand. "Jacob. Good to meet you."

Clint nodded and motioned over his shoulder. "This is my brother, Davie."

Davie shifted from foot-to-foot, dressed in only a stained white t-shirt, jeans, and a ball cap with a well-worn, bent bill.

He crossed his arms against the cold, exposing a faded tattoo on his right shoulder. "Hey."

"Sorry, dear. I should have introduced you to everyone." She gestured to her left. "This is Francois and Rosana."

Rosana's nightgown showed from under her hooded jacket. She held her long, dark hair in a loose ponytail at her shoulder, and her free arm tight across her body. Francois' belly parted his t-shirt and sweatpants and poked through the front of his open parka. The pair huddled together, nodded in unison, and Francois smiled wide.

Davie scratched at the patchy stubble on his cheek. "Looks like the power's out everywhere."

"Phones too." Rosana nestled closer to Francois. "Landlines and cell."

Penny pulled on the cuffs of her gloves. "There isn't even a signal on the radio."

Jacob looked around. "Any idea what's going on?"

Clint pointed toward his brother. "Davie said he saw something."

"I told you I did, Clint. I thought there was an earthquake or something. The walls of the camper were shaking and everything. When I looked out, I saw a big cloud of smoke, then the power went out."

Jacob turned to the south. A strange glow lit the horizon, but darkness blanketed Fort Erie. "Think it was Buffalo?"

"I know it was Buffalo. I know it." Davie adjusted his cap, and tucked a stray clutch of dull, brown hair behind his ear.

"Maybe the power station or something?"

Clint took a long drag from his cigarette and blew smoke to one side. "Not sure. Must have been something big to knock everything out over here, too."

Penny held the collar of her sweater tight around her neck.

"I'm sure the power will be back on before you know it, no need to worry."

"Either way, I'm heading in." Clint started toward his house, dragging his heavy boots in the snow. "Come on, Davie."

"See ya later, guys." Davie hopped after his brother, following the cleared path.

"We should be heading in as well. I'm freezing." Gwen put a hand on Penny's shoulder. "Stay warm, everyone."

Jacob glanced toward the house. "Oh no."

"What's wrong, dear?"

"The generator. I forgot to check it over. I'm not sure it's even hooked up."

"Well, we've already got a fire going, and I'm sure we could make some space for you."

"No, it's okay." Jacob sighed. "I'll figure something out."

"If you change your mind, you know where we'll be."

"Thanks, Gwen."

Rosana grabbed Francois by the arm and turned him to face their house. "Come on, love, we should get back inside too." Rosana glanced back to Jacob and gave a sly smile. "Very nice to meet you, Jacob."

Jacob's lips pinched into a strained grin, and warmth flooded his cold cheeks. As the sensation faded, he turned to watch the falling snow. An errant flake fell onto his eye. He dropped his head and blinked away the moisture. When he looked up, he found himself alone in the circle. With his hands in his jacket pockets, he followed his own tracks back to the porch, then swept his boot across the stair treads to clear them with each step up.

Jacob kicked off his boots and entered the kitchen. He took the flashlight from the kitchen table and clicked the button. A thin stream of yellow light guided him to the front closet. On the top shelf, he found an old toque with a curling bonspiel logo on the front and a pompom on top. He held the flashlight under his arm and pulled the toque over his head. Next, he went down the hall to his bedroom closet and pulled down a pile of folded blankets. He picked out two that did not feel like they had been made of straw and spread them over the bed. Dropping his coat on the floor, he crawled under the covers, otherwise clothed.

Jacob closed his eyes and tugged the blankets over his head. It took some time for sleep to take him. It was more than just the cold, though. An unformed thought played in the back of his mind. A sense of dread. A sense that the brewing storm and the falling snow would just be the beginning.

FIFTEEN

Alex knocked on the door of apartment 208 and stepped back. He shook melting snow from his coat and glanced along the hall. The pale shades of the vintage themed lights were dark. Paintings, in ornate frames, lined the walls. They reminded Alex of something you would see in the house of someone who appreciated art.

The door opened almost as far as the drawn chain would allow. An eye scanned through the crack. It settled on Alex, then widened. The door closed. Alex heard the chain release.

When the door opened next, it bounced back against the stop. A woman a few inches shorter than Alex, but with the same golden hair, wrapped her arms around him in a tight hug. "Where have you been? I expected you hours ago."

Alex returned the gesture, resting his cheek against her head. "Hi, Mom."

Alex's mother took a step back but held his shoulders with outstretched arms. "I was so worried. The phones…"

"I know, I wanted to call, but—"

"Is everything okay? I mean, out there. How did you even get here?"

Alex's eyes darted back and forth along the hall. "I'll explain inside."

Her gaze flitted around Alex. "But…wait, where's your friend?"

The door on the opposite side of the hall creaked open. They turned their attention to the face, half-concealed by the slab of stained wood.

A voice gruff and shaky with age called out. "Everything all right, Eileen?"

Alex traced the shadows on the man's face down to the ever-so-slight tremble in his jaw.

"Everything's fine, Cy. This is my boy, Alex. I've told you about him before."

The skeptical gray eye looked Alex over, then the man nodded. He faded back and closed the door.

Alex picked up the canvas bag from beside his feet. "Please, let's go inside."

Eileen's eyebrows furrowed. She nodded and made her way back into her apartment. Alex turned sideways through the door, following after her. He rested his bag beside an unused plastic boot mat, locked the deadbolt, and fastened the chain.

"Can I get you a water or a pop? I'm afraid I don't have much to offer, what with the power being out and all."

Alex stood in the entryway with his hands in his pockets. "Yeah, water would be good."

Eileen nodded. "Go get yourself set up in the spare room."

"Okay. Thanks, Mom."

Alex set his bag inside the bedroom door. Stepping slow, he kept his eyes on the floor as he moved along the side of the bed and up to the window. With the curtains pulled to one side, he leaned toward the glass. Boot tracks from his arrival had already started to fill in.

The harsh glow of staccato red and blue lights neared from around the corner. A police cruiser trudged along the middle of the street, fighting for traction. Another came soon after, its engine roaring as it went. Muffled sounds of shouting carried through the darkness.

Alex's hand fell away from the curtain. The pulsing lights continued past the complex and disappeared. Alex released his breath and turned to the darkened room.

SIXTEEN

When Jacob woke later that morning, it was to gentle wisps of his breath rising above him. He put on the thickest pair of socks he could find and added a sweater under his jacket. He wandered out to the kitchen, inspected the room, and scratched at his head. In many ways, he enjoyed the freedom that came with his self-imposed isolation, but not being able to heat up something to eat was a little much.

He moved to the kitchen window and peered past the curtains. Through the snow and frost, he noticed activity in the circle. Jacob made his way down the porch steps. For some reason, it felt warmer outside than it did in the house. The clouds were dense, but the falling snow had tapered off. Jacob looked to the smoke drifting from many of the chimneys in the circle. He wondered how his experience would be different if his grandfather had not replaced the wood-burning fireplace with an electric unit years before.

All the houses sat dark, as if the world were simply sleeping. The exception being the Miller's. Soft light glowed behind the drawn curtains. With no sign of a running generator, Jacob assumed they had a healthy supply of candles.

The same group from the night before lingered in the circle, and by the looks of it, they had a busy morning. A space ten meters across had been cleared of deep snow. At the end, toward the road, a fire burned. Both picnic tables had been dug out, and a few camp chairs sat arranged around the fire. Shoveled paths lead to each of the occupied houses.

A woman joined them from the back of the circle. Her eyes shimmered, and her rosy cheeks rounded when she smiled. A toddler followed her down the path from their home. Erica, and Parker, if Jacob remembered correctly. Hayden squirmed in her arms, scarf wrapped snug around his head.

Jacob half-raised a hand in greeting. "Morning everyone."

Gwen sidled up to him and slipped her arm through his. "Nice toque. How'd you sleep?"

"Okay, I guess." He looked down to his bare wrist. "What time is it, anyway?"

Clint stepped away from the fire and hooked his thumbs in his pockets. "It's almost nine."

"Wow, been a while since I've slept in that late."

"Want some coffee?" Clint reached for an enamel pot sitting next to the flames.

"Sure." Jacob scouted around for a cup.

"Here you go." Davie held out an oversized pink mug with a faded teddy bear on one side.

Jacob accepted it with a smile. "Thanks."

Clint poured the mug three-quarters full. Jacob joined those standing closer to the fire. Dancing around the group, a young girl in a puffy purple jacket sang a song about a chimpanzee eating cupcakes. She stopped in front of Jacob and fell silent. Through the clutch of wild hair hanging in her face, huge gray-blue eyes locked onto his. "Cheese is poisonous to coconuts." Before Jacob could respond, she resumed her song and skipped away.

Gwen giggled. "That little Allena, what a sweetheart."

Jacob downed a swig from the big pink mug. It was bitter and gritty, but he was happy to have something warm to drink. "So, any news?"

"Nothing yet." Francois stuck his chin out in a scowl. "Still cut off."

"Weird."

"It's a little warmer at least."

"Seems that way, but still, when's the last time you remember it being this cold?"

Gwen stepped away from Jacob and nestled her hands into her coat. "Not sure, been a few years. Anyway, I'm going to check on Harold and Penny. She said she wanted to keep him company. Let's all meet back out here in about fifteen minutes, I want to make sure everyone is in good shape. Even if the power comes back soon, I think it's going to be a long day." Gwen waved toward Jacob and then the fire. "There's some porridge if you're hungry. It's instant, but it does the trick. Might as well use it up."

SEVENTEEN

Alex left the spare bedroom, pulling his shirt down over his chest. Plush slippers slid across the oak floor. He stopped where the short hall opened and rubbed at one eye.

"Mom?" Alex scanned the dining and living room as he waited for a response. He leaned back and looked toward the bedrooms, then frowned and went into the living room. At the picture window, swirling snow obscured the details of the street below. Unable to discern much of anything, he sat on the end seat of the couch with his elbow up on the arm.

Alex jerked his head, and his eyes opened wide with the solid click of the front door closing. Eileen strolled through the kitchen with her jacket in her hand. "It's about time you were up. How did you sleep?"

Alex stifled a yawn. "Could have been better. A lot of racket out in the street last night."

Eileen pursed her lips and shrugged. "Kids have nothing better to do other than make a nuisance of themselves, I suppose. I tried to get some details, but Amy wasn't out yet.

Even in an outage, that woman hears things you wouldn't believe."

"Where were you, anyway?"

Eileen hugged her coat tight and angled her eyes away. "I was out for a smoke."

Alex sat tall. "When did you start again?"

"Oh, I don't know. After I moved in, the neighbors would invite me out for a chat. Everyone else was, so…"

"What, are you in high school?"

Eileen lowered her jacket and waved her son away as she entered her bedroom. "I'm a grown woman, Alex."

Alex crossed his arms, and his shoulders dropped.

Returning to the living room, Eileen perched on the arm of the couch opposite Alex. "Hungry?"

"I guess so."

"I'll make some peanut butter and banana sandwiches if you can go across the hall and grab the coffee."

Alex raised an eyebrow. "Sorry?"

"Cy. He's making us coffee."

"How?"

"Oh. He's got a gas stove to boil the water. That still works, at least. The rest, well, Cy is sort of an aficionado. He makes his coffee in one of those press things. Has an old-fashioned hand crank grinder too." Eileen rose and tugged on her fleece pullover. "He said it'd be ready when we need it."

Alex heaved a sigh. "Okay."

With Eileen fussing in the kitchen, Alex pushed himself up from the couch and shuffled toward the front door.

Across the hall, he rapped on the wood frame three times and waited to one side. Sluggish feet trudged behind the secured door. They paused, then locks and deadbolts clicked free, one after the other. The door creaked open, but the space inside was empty. Alex leaned across to see better.

"Come on then. I'll be in the kitchen."

Alex instinctively looked both ways along the hall, then squeezed through the half-open doorway. The latch clicked home, but he turned the knob to make sure it had not somehow locked. The air inside was heavy with humidity and must. Sparse furnishings lined the walls. Black and white photographs, in tarnished metal frames, crowded the top of the sideboard in the living room.

In the galley kitchen, Cy braced himself against the laminate countertop and poured from a pot of steaming water. Dark grounds swirled and muddied in a glass cylinder. The scent of fresh coffee wafted throughout the small space. Cy extended a steady hand to a silver lid resting on the counter. Twisting it down, he pushed the French press in Alex's direction. "Give it a couple minutes. Then..." He circled a boney finger around the knob on top of the lid.

"Will do." Alex slid a foot forward, stretched his arm to take the handle of the press, then turned to go.

"Which one are you?"

Alex stopped and steadied his hand under the bottom of the coffee press. He glanced over his shoulder. "Pardon?"

"Which one are you? The oldest, or the younger one?"

Alex let out his held breath and raised his eyebrows. He turned to face Cy. "The younger."

Cy stuck out his lower lip and nodded. "Your mother talks about you all the time. Not so much about your brother."

Alex cleared his throat.

"You're a cop?"

"Not anymore."

"Didn't work out for ya?"

"No."

Cy watched Alex's eyes, then he grasped the handle of a cane hanging on the edge of the counter. Setting it on the floor, he adjusted his stance and returned his focus to Alex. "You know what's going on?" He pointed a finger toward the ceiling. "The lights and such."

"No idea."

Cy sniffed and broke his gaze. "Best be getting back. Coffee's about ready."

Alex hesitated, his jaw slack. "Yeah. Thanks." He spun forty-five degrees and marched to the door.

Back in his mother's apartment, Alex set the French press down on the kitchen counter and continued to the living room. Eileen positioned two sandwiches on the cutting board in front of her. Her eyes followed Alex as he went. "Everything okay?"

Arms crossed, Alex stood in front of the big window. "Sure."

Eileen watched her son as she wiped her hands on a dish towel. "Come on, sit at the table. I'll bring everything out."

Alex ran a hand through his hair. He sat at the round, white-painted dining table. Eileen set the cutting board and a short stack of napkins down at the center. Re-emerging from the kitchen, she put the steaming coffee press on the table and slowly pushed the knob down, collecting the grounds to the bottom. "Probably going to be a little strong."

Alex adjusted himself in his seat and pinched his flat hands between his knees. "It's okay. I like it that way."

Eileen poured coffee into two plain mugs, then placed each sandwich on a napkin and slid one in front of Alex. "Go on, eat up." She lifted her sandwich and nibbled on the bottom corner.

Alex took his sandwich in one hand. Twisting it back and forth, he inspected each side, then took a healthy bite from the top. He set it down, swept the falling crumbs into his cupped hand, and deposited them in the napkin. Still chewing, he shifted his weight forward on his crossed arms.

"What's going on?"

"Nothing." Alex sighed and lowered his eyes to the table. "I mean…I don't know."

"I'm sure everything will be back to normal before you know it."

"Yeah." Alex straightened the paper towel, ensuring it was square with the edge of the table.

Eileen sipped from her mug and winced, then held it propped up with her elbows resting on either side of her sandwich. "How's Ivy been?"

Alex picked up his sandwich, then set it back down. "Not sure. Haven't talked to her in a while."

Eileen frowned. "I'm sorry, hon. You two seemed to be doing so well."

Alex shrugged at her response. He wanted to tell her about their fights over being dismissed from the force, or the night of his last birthday party, but did not. "Some things aren't meant to be."

"That's what Grandpa used to say. Was also a fan of 'when God closes a door, he opens a window'."

"Which is weird, since the only other time I heard him mention God was when he'd curse."

The seriousness on Eileen's face relented into a chuckle. "You're right there."

A smile pulled at the corner of Alex's lips. He palmed his sandwich and bit off what remained of the top.

Eileen drained her coffee and set the mug down. "After

breakfast, I figured we could have a bit of a read, like the old days. I've been a little spend happy at the bookstore lately, so there's lots of options."

"Sure, that sounds nice."

Eileen patted Alex's hand. "Good." With a warm smile, she picked up her sandwich and took another bite.

EIGHTEEN

Glowing embers crackled as they burned. Jacob scraped the last of the oatmeal from his bowl. Gwen sauntered down the path to the circle in a pair of her heaviest boots and a brimmed wool hat.

"Looking good, Gwen." Clint grinned and flicked the butt end of his cigarette into the fire.

Gwen shrugged. "Hey, a girl's got to do what a girl's got to do." She warmed her hands over the fire. "All right then, did anyone have a chance to check their supplies? Clint?"

"We should be okay. I doubt there'll be a shortage of blankets and stuff. I've got to dig out our camping gear, the heater and that. The kids are getting cranky about the cold."

Allena dug holes in the snow nearby. She raised her head but stayed focused on the task at hand. "It's not s'posed to be cold in the house, Daddy."

"I know, baby, I'm working on it." Clint rubbed his hat against his forehead. "See what I mean? I'm just hoping we have enough propane to get us through."

"What about food? We just stocked up on water and anything in a can. Lots to go around if need be."

"Yesterday was payday, and Erica made a trip to the grocery store, so we're good there. I'm worried about how long the milk and such will last. I was thinking of packing some snow in the fridge to help keep the temperature down."

"Not a bad idea, actually. Rosana, what about you guys?"

Rosana brushed her hair back. "I'm sure we'll be fine." She wrapped her arm around Francois and snuggled into his shoulder. "If there are troubles with the fireplace, we have other ways to keep warm."

"That's good then." Gwen turned away, rolling her eyes. "Anyone heard from those two in the corner?"

"I knocked on their door this morning." Francois set his hand over Rosana's. "Nicolas told me they were doing okay. Said he'd be out in a bit to chat."

"What about the Millers?"

"You know George. Looks like he's got things under control."

"I'm sure he does." Gwen relaxed her arms and turned her back to the fire. "Well, as long as Penny and I stay warm, we'll make it. We've got Harold all set up too."

Davie adjusted his ball cap and slid his hands in the back pockets of his jeans. "So, that's it? We're just going to sit around and wait for this to be over?"

"What exactly do you propose we do, dear?"

"I don't know. There's got to be something. How long do you think this'll last?"

"That's hard to say."

"I mean, you'd figure that the town would be out to clear the roads at some point, right? They're not gonna just leave us stranded out here, are they?"

Clint dug the heel of his boot into the ground and folded his arms across his chest. "Hell, they ain't coming close enough to us to make a difference. I think we need to try to get out ourselves."

Gwen raised her chin. "Does that mean you're volunteering, dear?"

"Sure, why not. Got the only vehicle with enough ground clearance to try the road out." Clint smiled wide. "Plus, it'll be fun."

Davie perked up. "Hey, Clint, can I drive? Just to the main road?"

"No way in hell you're driving my truck, Davie. You should know that."

"Aw, come on, man. When am I gonna get another chance like this?"

"Not happening."

Davie flung a rude gesture at Clint with a sour expression on his face, then turned away.

Nicolas descended the path from his house with his tan wool trench coat buttoned to the top of his neck. He smoothed a hand through glossy black hair, graying at the temples, greeting the group with a nod.

Francois patted him on the back. "Hello, Nick. How are you holding up?"

"I'm okay. Malena is…" He twisted a flat hand back and forth and frowned. "You know?"

"Comme ci, comme ça?"

Nicolas smiled and pushed the wire-framed glasses up on his nose. "Yes, I believe so."

Francois laughed.

Nicolas moved toward the fire and held out his hand. "You must be Jacob. Nice to meet you."

Jacob rose out of his chair to shake hands. "Nicolas. Hi. Good to meet you."

"Okay, so Clint is going to try and head into town." Gwen looked back to her house. "I'm thinking we should all fill some jugs with water. Everything is still running now, but you never know what's going to happen."

Francois scratched at the short cropped salt-and-pepper scruff. "We should stock up on firewood, too."

Clint motioned over his shoulder. "Chainsaw's in the back of the truck. I'll drop it off with one of the kid's sleds, and an axe or two, if you want to go for a run while we're out."

Nicolas raised his hand. "I can help with that, if you like."

Francois gave a thumb's up and smiled. "Appreciate it, friend. There's a few dead trees just out back of our place, so we shouldn't have to go far."

"Good, I think we're set, then." Gwen paused and snapped her fingers. "Oh, Jacob, you haven't got your generator situation figured out yet, have you?"

Jacob leaned forward and held his hands toward the fire. "No, guess I should go have a look."

"Better hurry, dear. I get the feeling there's more on the way."

Clint trudged toward his house. "I'll be right back with the saw and the sled. Let's go, Davie."

"Yeah, yeah. I'm coming." Davie scowled and followed his brother.

Jacob set his empty bowl down on the nearest picnic table. He leaned back against the wood top and watched the falling snow mingle with the rising smoke from the fire. His mind wandered, going over the mental checklist of what the generator would need, and to what else he might be forgetting.

———

Jacob lifted a package of sliced ham and sniffed it. He removed three slices, stacked them on a piece of dry white bread, and added a slice of processed cheese. With another piece of bread on top, he pressed the sandwich down with a flat hand. Jacob picked it up and bit into the soft bread. Leaning forward, he balanced on his elbow and stared at the butter dish sitting an arm's length away. A bent knife and a few rogue chunks of butter sat on the counter next to it. He took another bite of the sandwich, grabbed an open can of beans from the opposite side of the sink, and headed outside.

Davie sat alone by the fire. He poked at the smoldering coals with a thick branch. Jacob set the can close to the fire and parked himself in a chair two seats over. Davie tossed the ashen branch to one side and looked up to Jacob. "Hey, man."

"Hey."

Davie reclined in his chair and pulled at the bottom of his baggy jean jacket. It covered a thick plaid jacket underneath. "That your lunch?"

Jacob nodded. "It is."

"But, it's almost dinnertime."

"Yeah, well, generator took longer than I thought."

Davie frowned and nodded. He motioned to the can by the fire. "Just like in the old days, like a cowboy on the range."

"Not much of a choice. I can put up with a lot, but cold beans aren't one of them."

Davie chuckled. "We all have our limits, I guess." He reached into his denim coat pocket and tugged out an open package of hot dogs. Unrolling the loose end, he freed one from the plastic wrap. Half of it disappeared with his first bite.

Jacob scrunched up his face. "Really, man?"

"What?"

"Just, right out of the package like that?"

Davie chewed with a gaping mouth. "Nothing wrong with it. They're cooked, you know."

"I guess…"

"Besides, I can't find the roasting sticks." Davie popped the last piece in his mouth and put the package back into his jacket. "So, your generator is up and running?"

"Yeah."

"That's good."

Davie leaned back and ran his tongue across his teeth while he gave his surroundings a once-over. He sighed and took his phone from his pocket. Holding it out in front of him, he pressed down on the power button. The screen remained dark. He pressed it again.

"Everything okay?"

"Not really. Battery's dead."

"Is that a big deal at the moment?"

"Just bored, that's all. I killed it playing games."

"Oh."

Davie scratched at his patchy chin. "How long do you think this will last?"

Jacob shrugged. "I don't know. Hopefully, not much longer. I mean, when I was a kid, I remember the power being out sometimes, but it was for a couple of days at best."

Davie frowned from one side of his mouth and let out a slow breath.

"What are you worried about?"

"Not sure. It's just, I saw when they came home the other day," Davie pointed in the direction of Gwen and Penny's house, "the whole back of the car was filled with toilet paper."

"What?"

"It's true. Stacked to the roof. I'm a little worried that if this goes on too long, I mean, what if we run out of shit tickets?"

His serious face broke, and Jacob laughed. "I'm pretty sure we'll be fine."

"I hope so." Davie heaved a sigh and tilted forward. "I'm going to go chop wood or something."

"All right, have fun with that."

"Sure. Enjoy your beans."

Jacob smiled. "Thanks."

Jacob chewed on the last bite of his sandwich and watched the fire. Crunching footsteps came from his left, and he glanced sideways.

"Hello, dear."

He wiped his mouth. "Hey, Gwen."

At the fire, Gwen bent down to set a pot of water on the simmering coals. "Get everything sorted, did ya?"

Jacob, tepid beans in hand, shrugged. "I hope so."

Gwen gave a tight smile as she gathered two fresh cut logs from the wood pile. "Looks like you're taken care of, but if you need dinner, I'm putting a little something together."

"Thanks, I think I'll eat my beans and head in. I have some tidying up to do, and I'd like to make it an early night."

Gwen nodded. "Understandable." She smacked her gloves together to purge them of tree bark and snow. "Well, you know where we are if you need anything. If not, have yourself a good night."

Spooning a mouthful of beans, Jacob waved his thanks.

Gwen patted a hand on Jacob's shoulder as she strode past. "Night, dear."

NINETEEN

Mati eased the front door of an older bungalow shut and stepped out onto the porch. Dim light flickered through sheer, red curtains over the front window beside it. Sam sat at attention on the bottom porch step, her ears perked. Mati scratched at the top of her head on the way by.

Halfway down the snow-covered front walk, the door creaked open. Mati stopped in her tracks and glanced back as Sam moved close to her side. Jessie propped himself up against the peeling door frame and tucked his hands beneath his folded arms. "Where you goin'?"

Mati's expression stayed flat. "Just need to get some air."

"Hey, it's all good." Jessie hunched his shoulders. "When you get back, maybe we can, you know, hang out?" His eyes were clear like glass. "Have some fun."

Mati's hand moved to the strap of the bag over her shoulder, but she held fast, not wanting to draw attention to it. "Sure, I won't be long. You know, it's...cold."

Jessie tightened his grip on himself and peered to the sky.

"Yeah." He redirected his gaze to Mati and gave a crooked smile. "I'll be in the basement when you get back."

Mati's lips went thin, and she lowered her head in a reluctant nod.

"Cool." Jessie kept his eyes on Mati as he backed into the darkened house and out of sight behind the closed door.

Mati turned away from the house and raised her face to the sky. Swirling white flakes brushed against her warm cheeks and stuck to moisture accumulating at her eyes. Without speaking, she stepped to the sidewalk, turned left, and continued down the block with Sam right behind her.

TWENTY

Jacob stacked the last of the cut wood on the edge of the circle near the fire, then lifted his hat and wiped at his brow with the back of his hand. His limbs ached. More so, after spending the morning foraging with Francois.

Dense cloud cover obscured the sun. Fresh snow fell, but it did not amount to much. One of Gwen's cats stalked prey off to the north. Jacob assumed it also heard the birds chirping behind Clint's place.

Francois came up beside him and crossed his arms. "All done?"

"Yeah, finally."

"Good, good." Francois eyed the pile of firewood. "You know, if we have to start going out much further, we might need to pack a lunch."

Jacob smiled. "Yeah, it's surprising how much we're going through."

Francois surveyed the area around them. Scrunching his face, he let out a deep breath. "Do you ever get tired of the snow?"

"What?"

"You know. Tired of it. Like, it makes you angry just to look at it."

"Oh," Jacob smirked, "no, not really. It's a pain in the ass, I guess. Seriously though, we get a few feet, lose electricity, and we're completely useless."

Francois sneered. "Stupid bloody snow." He pulled his gloves off and crammed them in his back pocket. "Listen, I'll go stash the sled, then I'm going to head in and clean up."

"Sure, sounds like a plan. I'll head in too. Promise I won't take all the hot water."

Francois grinned. "Very kind of you." He lifted the rope attached to the sled and lead it along the path to Clint's house.

Jacob picked up a small saucepan from one of the picnic tables, knelt beside a simmering stock pot on the fire, and dipped it in. He brought it out nearly full and carefully walked the hot water to his kitchen counter.

He grabbed a tea towel from the handle of the oven door, dipped it in the steaming saucepan, and twisted it to release most of the water. He buffed a bar of soap against it, then scrubbed at his face and hair, holding his breath as the warmth absorbed into his skin. With his shirt pulled up, he rubbed at his chest and armpits. Flipping the towel to the clean side, he wiped himself down. A second towel dried his skin and took most of the chill away. He tossed the used towels into one side of the sink and poured the murky water down the drain of the other. After dressing in fresh clothes, he took the saucepan back out to the circle.

Gwen crouched by the fire to adjust the coffee pot on the coals. As Jacob neared, she raised her eyes over the frames of her glasses. "Good morning, dear. How'd you sleep last night?"

"Better than the night before, that's for sure. It's nice to have heat again."

"I bet." Gwen stood and brushed her hands along her pantlegs.

She added a small log to the fire and pulled a chair beside Jacob. They watched the flames, listening to the hisses and pops. Gwen smiled and settled back. "This is sort of nice, isn't it? I mean, besides the power being out and all. There's not much to worry about, really, just what's in front of you."

"I don't know, I think of it more like forced camping," Jacob sighed, "and I don't like camping."

Gwen laughed and clasped her hands together. "Well, I'm afraid you don't have much of a choice, my boy."

Jacob smiled. "Yeah, I know."

Penny came down the path from Harold's house. A winter jacket and thick scarf were wrapped tight over her plush housecoat. She untucked one arm and waved her hand as she neared the circle. "Good morning."

"Morning, Penny."

"Coffee ready? Harold wants a cup."

"It's on the fire, should be almost to his liking."

"Perfect, thank you." Penny chose a mug from one of the picnic tables, brushed a dusting of snow off, and filled it just shy of the rim.

Gwen leaned one elbow on the arm of her chair. "Let me know if he's hungry, and I'll get some breakfast started."

"Oh, you know how he is. Won't need much, but I'm sure he's ready to eat any time."

"I'll have something for him shortly."

"Sounds good, I'll let him know." Penny fixed her gaze on the mug held out in front of her and shuffled along the path to Harold's front door.

Gwen laid back in her chair. "So, anything special on the agenda for today?"

"Not really. Generator is running good so far. We should be okay for firewood for a bit. I keep thinking I need to get ready for work tomorrow, but with the way things are looking, that won't be necessary."

"I would suggest it probably won't."

"Not much I can do. Still feels weird that I can't at least call in to let someone know."

"Don't worry, dear. They're all in the same spot we are. More or less."

———

The bark of a big V8 punched a hole through the crisp, still air over the community. Jacob turned to see Clint climb up the front tire of his truck and sweep packed snow from the windshield with a gloved hand.

Clint said he liked the way it sounded. Jacob had not heard anyone else share the same opinion, but the rotted-out mufflers fit the theme. Clint's truck appeared as if it had not seen a car wash since it drove off the lot. Rust broke through the faded cobalt paint on nearly every panel. The beat up and twisted bush bumper on the front hung crooked from too few bolts. The back bumper went missing years before. Spotlights mounted to the headache rack pointed in every direction except forward, including the one on the end with a broken lens. Jacob had not previously given it much thought, but he grew concerned that the ragged and neglected machine might be their only way out.

———

Jacob twisted the cap tight on a small red gas can. He looked up to agitated voices coming from the road into the community. Two men trudged along the deep tracks that Clint's truck had left on the way out. The falling snow had eased, but it still obscured them as they neared. Jacob spit, the taste of gasoline burning his mouth, then stood. He assumed siphoning would be easy. Lesson learned.

Around the fire in the greenspace, Gwen, Francois, and Nicolas watched up the lane. As the pair advanced, the bickering became clear. Francois dropped his shoulders, waved a hand toward them, and turned to the fire.

"Jesus Christ, I'm frozen half to death."

"Quit your bitchin', Davie. Maybe, if you'd of worn something more than a shitty pair of sneakers, it wouldn't be so bad."

"Maybe, if some jackass knew how to drive his big, bad fuckin' truck, I wouldn't have to be walking through three fuckin' feet of snow right now."

"Jesus, that's all I've heard for the last half hour. Say it one more time, and I'll punch your fuckin' teeth in."

"Sure, you will."

"*Try me.*"

Davie saw the venom in Clint's eyes and closed his lips tight.

Gwen shuffled forward as they approached the group. "What happened, boys?"

"This dick head—"

"Don't even start. I swear to Christ, you're gonna get it."

"Whatever. I'm going to go get some dry clothes. You can tell them what a shitty driver you are."

Clint swung out with both hands open. Davie ducked, bringing his arms up over his head, and scurried away.

"Lucky I didn't leave you in the ditch, you little prick."

Davie flashed his middle finger and stuck his tongue out at Clint, then turned and ran for his camper.

Gwen's eyebrows pinched together, and she held her hands on her hips. "Are you about done?"

Clint let out a long, slow exhale. "Sorry. It's bad enough we got stuck without the cry baby yapping about it all the way home."

Francois stepped forward with a steaming mug in his hands. "Here, warm up a little, then you can tell us what happened."

"Thanks." Clint smiled and downed half the contents of the mug. "Damn, that is rough." He caught Gwen glaring at him. "Sorry, it's just…sorry. Anyway, it wasn't too bad until right before the big bend heading to the main road. I hit a drift, and it sucked us into the ditch. I tried to get it out, but that son of a bitch ain't goin' nowhere. Not even a decent tree or anything to winch it out."

"Did you see anyone else while you were out?"

"Main road is deserted, as far as I could see. It's kinda creepy how quiet it is out there. On the way back, I got a good look up toward the Benson's place. They're trying to clear the driveway, but they were a'ways off. Davie was bitching so much, I just wanted to get back."

"Guess that means we're stuck."

"I don't know. I think we might be able to get out to the highway if we geared up."

Francois shrugged and looked to the north. "Might be worth a try. It's not that far."

"Far enough. It shouldn't be too bad, but it will take a while, and I've had enough of walking through ass-deep snow for one day. Let's give it a shot in the morning."

"So, what do we do now?"

Gwen scratched at her forehead. "Well, I guess it's almost lunchtime. Let's get something to eat, and then get ready for another night in the cold."

TWENTY-ONE

Alex snapped the back cover of the book shut and set it down on the arm of the couch. He relaxed his arms and sank back into the soft cushions.

"How was it?"

Alex looked through the living room window and shrugged. "All right, I guess. Not as good as the reviews made it out to be."

Eileen twisted her lips and watched Alex over the top of her glasses. "Reviews are all paid for, anyway. Can't trust anything with a marketing budget behind it."

"True." Alex lowered his eyes to the street below. "It actually doesn't look too bad out there."

Eileen broke her attention away from the novel in her hand to take a quick glimpse out the window. She made an agreeable noise and went back to reading.

Alex pushed himself upright. "I think I'm going to go out for a quick walk. Maybe see if I can get to the creek."

"Be careful. Probably won't get much help if you fall in."

Alex's expression soured. "I'm not going to fall in, Mom."

Eileen shrugged, but kept her eyes on her book. "Hey, you never know."

Alex strode off toward the bedrooms.

"Take my coat. It's nice and warm," she looked to Alex over the top of her glasses, "and don't worry, it's good for ladies or men."

"I brought my gear. It's all down in the car."

"Then take mine and bring your stuff up on your way back."

Alex stopped with one hand on the corner leading to the bedrooms. "You sure? After I drown, you might not get it back."

Eileen smiled. "I'll just have to buy another one with your life insurance money."

Alex snorted and rolled his eyes. "Thanks, Mom."

———

With his mother's coat zipped to his chin, Alex pushed through the first set of exterior doors and paused in the space between. He slipped a pair of gloves on, then pressed on the lock bar of the next set and moved into the cold.

Two women stood in the corner, one on either side of the smoking urn. Alex acknowledged them with a thin-lipped nod. They stared back with vacant eyes. Alex stretched his chin over the collar and started toward the parking lot.

"Isn't that Eileen's coat?"

Alex stopped and eyed the pair. "Yeah, I borrowed it. I'm her son."

The woman on the left took a drag from her cigarette and pushed the hood back from her head. She narrowed her eyes and looked Alex up and down. "Right. I heard you showed up last night. It's a little small on you, by the way."

Alex cocked his head. "Any chance you would be Amy?"

"One and the same." She finished her smoke with a long drag, then crushed the butt end into the urn. "And you are?"

"Alex."

"Pleasure." Amy's hands retreated into her sleeves. "Where are you off to, anyway?"

"Nowhere in particular. Wanted to get out for a bit."

"Yeah, well, watch yourself. Something bad's going on, some kind of mess down at the border. Far too many uniforms with big guns wandering around for my liking."

"What, like the cops?"

"For a start. Military started showing up a while ago, and some others I'm not sure about yet."

"Oh."

"Well, good luck with your walk." Amy set off for the warmth of the foyer. Her silent partner pushed out her own cigarette and followed along.

"Thanks."

Alex stepped into the deeper snow and continued across the lot. He stopped at the farthest visitor spot to check on the rental. After swiping a hand to clear the side window, he put his face close to the glass. The interior was unchanged from when he parked the day before, so he moved on.

At the main road, Alex checked both ways before crossing. Deep grooves carved through the snow in both directions, crisscrossing and merging in the middle. No vehicles, military or otherwise, could be seen. He proceeded along the road and made his way down a narrow one-way street. Frigid wind bit at his face, chilling him to the bone.

The road came to a T, and he stopped again. His legs

burned. The creek was still another block away. To the west, towering apartment buildings loomed over the frozen sliver of water. A police cruiser, lights flashing, sat bookended by two matte black Humvees. Five or six figures in dark uniforms huddled around them. Alex weaved down a street to his right, plowing tracks in the snow along the way.

As Alex drew near, one from the group focused on him and stepped away from the others. He jogged into the street with one hand at the rifle strapped to his body and the other held out flat toward Alex. A few paces away he stopped. "Sir, the city has been put under a state of emergency with an order for everyone to shelter in place. Please return to your residence."

Alex scanned the soldier's fatigues for a sign of rank, then looked past him to the parking lot. On the opposite side of the vehicles, he caught a glimpse of what looked like bodies covered in white sheets. Red stains littered the snow. "What's going on?"

"The city is under a state of emergency. You need to return to your home."

"What branch are you?"

"Go home, sir."

Alex planted himself firm and held the soldier's gaze.

The soldier rubbed his chapped lips together and swallowed. Even though it was well below freezing, perspiration beaded on his forehead. "Last chance. Go home. Please. It will be dark soon."

Alex's jaw tightened. When he looked again to the vehicles, he noticed the troop of soldiers watching him. Not wanting to push his luck, he relented and swiveled to trek back home.

TWENTY-TWO

A dull roar reverberated through the walls. Alex sat up in bed and rubbed at his eyes. When he looked to the window, an orange glow dimmed and disappeared behind the drawn curtains. Pulling off the covers, he swung his legs to the hardwood floor. Uncoordinated feet bumped an empty liquor bottle, and hollow glass rolled away. His mother kept the few bottles of hard liquor on hand hidden, but the apartment was not that big.

He stumbled forward, searching his hand to the exterior wall for support. With his face close to the glass, ragged breath pulsed fog across the pane. Alex fought to focus on the scene below through drooping eyelids. He yanked the window open a few inches and hunched with one arm crossed over his chest.

Indistinct noise echoed along the frozen street. A bright flash, then a pop. Another rang out in the distance. Alex looked to each side of the window. Shallow breath, in short bursts, came through pinched lips. On the second attempt, he grasped the edge of the window and slid it shut.

His body turned away from the commotion outside, and a moment too late, his eyes followed. His knee caught a corner of the bed, and like a mannequin falling to pieces, he collapsed.

"Shit."

Reddened cheek flat against the floor, he reached out to prop himself up. Groping at the blankets on the bed for leverage, he pulled. With a slight miscalculation of weight, the blankets pooled on top of him, and he fell back on his face. Alex muttered another curse. He twisted on his side, sealing himself in a tangle of layers. Soon, his breathing steadied, and he slipped into a fitful sleep.

TWENTY-THREE

"Morning, dear."

"Morning." Jacob situated himself with his hands held over the fire. "How are things?"

"As well as can be expected."

"That's all right then?"

Gwen shrugged. "Any chance you heard something funny going on last night?"

"Not that I can remember. I had some really weird dreams, but I think I was out cold for the most part."

"Well, I didn't notice anything myself. Harold said there was something going on across the river, heard some commotion at the crossing maybe."

"Weird. I hope everything is okay."

Gwen set her hands at her sides. "I'm sure it's not a big deal, but it seemed to bother him a little more than he wanted to let on. Anyway, coffee's on if you're interested."

"Yeah, maybe." Jacob took an empty mug from the cluttered table, filled it from the enamel pot on the fire, then lowered himself into the chair next to Gwen. After a short sip, he held the mug by its handle and set it on his knee.

They sat, for a time, watching the fire in silence. Gwen noticed a break in the clouds overhead. A single beam of sunlight lit a path from the sky to the river. "Looks like we might be in for a decent day after all." Balancing on her elbow, she faced Jacob. "You know what? I think we need to do a proper cookout dinner tonight. Show this storm it hasn't beat us."

Jacob smiled at the thought. "Yeah, that sounds nice."

Gwen patted Jacob on his knee. "All right then, it's a date."

TWENTY-FOUR

Alex flipped a page, stared beyond the words for a moment, then set the book down on its face. He massaged his temples with his thumb and pointer finger.

Eileen looked up. "Are you okay?"

"Yeah, just a bit of a headache."

"I have some of those gel caps you like in the medicine cabinet."

Alex sighed. "Might as well." He made to stand but paused. He cocked his ear to the front door. "Did you hear that?"

"Hear what?"

Alex leaned to the edge of the couch. "I don't know. Like, a thump."

"Probably just the neighbors moving furniture or something."

Pushing himself to stand, Alex interlocked his fingers, stretched his arms high above his head, then set his hands on his hips. "I'll go have a look."

Focused on her story, Eileen mouthed an acknowledgment and turned to the next page.

Alex put his ear against the front door. Any noises he heard were dull and indistinct. He slowly drew back the chain and deadbolt, double-checked the peephole, then turned the knob. With one eye free of the door frame, Alex glanced along the hall.

A stocky man in a wild patterned jacket, with two large bags at his feet, paced in small circles. He held a heavy pair of gloves in his thick hand. The door of the apartment closest to him opened, and two other men came out into the hall. Both had jackets similar to the man waiting with the bags. One had a ski mask pulled up, showing a large nose and patchy complexion. The other had stringy, dark hair and a goatee to match. He set a small bag down next to the others.

Alex held his breath and his gaze when the group of men moved toward him. The one with the stringy hair tapped on the next closest apartment door. One arm hung straight by his side, and in the other, his fingers flexed around the handle of a semi-automatic pistol.

The door of apartment 206 opened, and a hushed greeting was spoken. The gunman wiped at his nose and gestured as if he wanted to enter. The hinges of the door creaked as it began to close. A leg snapped out to hold the door, and the gunman pushed inside, with the man in the mask following right behind. Alex heard muffled sounds of struggle, then the door slammed shut.

He shrank back and eased his own door closed. A rapid, uneven heartbeat thundered in his ears.

"Alex?"

Alex latched the chain and set both locks, then made his

way back to the living room. As he entered, Eileen looked up from the book on her lap. "What's wrong?"

Alex pointed a hand toward the front door. "I don't know. There's a group of guys. I think they're…"

Eileen stiffened. "Alex, what is it?"

"Just…keep your voice down. I'll deal with it."

Eileen's face grew hard, and her lips drew thin. "Maybe it's a misunderstanding. I'm sure—" An assertive knock came at the door. She turned shaky eyes to Alex.

Alex held a hand low and spoke in a hushed tone. "It's not a misunderstanding."

"It has to be." Eileen pushed herself up. "I'll show you."

Alex stepped in front of his mother. "*No.*"

The knock came again, but this time, stronger and louder. A muted voice sounded through the deep wooden door. "I can hear you in there."

Eileen locked eyes with her son.

Alex held a hand low. "Stay here."

He moved at a steady pace toward the door. His vision sharpened, the world around him became vivid. Holding the doorknob, he drew back the deadbolt, then planted his foot a few inches from the bottom of the door. Unbuttoning a sheath on his belt with his free hand, he removed a matte black folding knife and unhinged the blade. Alex kept his face half-hidden as he cracked the door open. "What can I do for you?"

The man with the gun glanced down the hall. "You can open the door, for a start."

"Not gonna happen."

"I can assure you, it's gonna happen, whether you like it or not."

"Listen, I don't give a shit what you're up to, but come in here, and you'll regret it."

The man cocked his head and licked at his crooked teeth. "Fuck you, tough guy. Open the door."

"I can't do that."

"You can, and you fuckin' will," the man waved the pistol, "or I'll put one in your thick skull."

Alex adjusted the knife in his hand.

The man pushed on the door, but it held. "Open the fuckin' door."

"No."

Laughing to himself, the man shook his head. "All right, you asked for it." He stepped back and raised his boot.

Two quick shots rang out. With the third, blood sprayed from the man's neck. His eyes froze wide open, and his body folded to the ground.

Across the hall, Cy stood in his open doorframe, the barrel of his shotgun pointed at the floor. He turned to check up the hall with wide eyes. Saying nothing, he looked back to Alex, stepped to one side, and closed his door with barely a click.

The man laid on the floor, grasping his throat and gurgling. Heavy footsteps brought a figure in a dark, mottled uniform. He towered over the dying man with the muzzle of his rifle trained on his head. Goggles and a facemask obscured the features of the soldier's face. A clear voice, despite the covering, directed an order. "Get back inside, sir."

With a quick nod, Alex stepped back to shut the door and leave him to his work.

"Wait." The soldier lifted the goggles to the top of his helmet and pulled down on his mask. "You're the guy from out in the road, right?"

Alex scanned the soldier's face. "Yes."

"You military or PD?"

Alex cocked his head. "Cop, once upon a time. How did you know?"

"I recognized the look in your eyes." The soldier ground his teeth, looked to the man writhing on the ground, then to Alex. "We're being told to pull back. The border was overrun last night."

Alex swallowed hard.

"Whatever you do, don't—"

Gunfire erupted on the floor below. The soldier readied his rifle. "Just, stay inside and keep your door locked."

"Wait, don't what?"

The soldier sighted his rifle at the man on the ground. Alex tensed and slammed the door. A single shot rang out in the hall, followed by the sound of something heavy being dragged away.

Alex glanced back to see his mother staring at him with her arms wrapped tight against her chest. "What was that, Alex? What happened?"

"We need to close the curtains."

Eileen nodded, then scurried to the living room.

Alex steadied his breath and held the doorknob, then eased the door open a crack. A dark, glossy stain marked the carpet, but no body remained. With the door pulled back enough to stick his head out, Alex surveyed both sides of the hall. It was empty, save for the two large bags on the floor toward the exit. As he backed inside, he noticed the pistol propped against the baseboard. Alex snatched it from the floor and slipped inside before locking the door.

He secured the knife in its sheath, then popped the clip of the gun. Fifteen rounds left and one in the chamber. He stuck the pistol into the back of his waistband and marched off to collect his gear.

———

Returning to his mother's apartment, Alex wiped his feet on the mat out of habit. His canvas bag sat beside the door, full to the point the zipper would not close all the way. Two folded blankets looped through the stiff handles. He shook his watch down his wrist to check it. He hoped they would have had more time.

"Alex?"

Alex leaned around the corner of the entryway. "I'm here."

His mother stood outside of her bedroom with a full bag in each hand. Her head tilted back, so she could see past the hood of her coat. "I packed everything you told me. I think I'm ready."

Alex gestured toward the door. "Okay, let's go."

In the hall, Alex took one slow step after another, only shifting focus from his surroundings to make sure his mother followed close behind. At the farthest end, he pressed an ear against the stairwell door. He turned to his mother and held a finger against his lips, then eased the door open.

Quiet breathing, and the tap of boots on the stairs, kept a steady rhythm as they descended. The heavy door of the lobby creaked open. Alex scanned the darkened space, then emerged from the doorway, holding his mother's hand tight. He led her past blood spatter and streaked handprints on the wall and around glistening stains in the carpet. In the foyer, Alex set his bag and one of his mother's down. "I'll go get the truck. Be ready to go, like we talked about, okay?" He looked back to the vacant lobby. "Don't touch anything while I'm gone."

Eileen nodded, staring out at the wash of white. "Why… why can't we bring anyone else? At least Cy, he—"

"No, Mom. We can't risk anyone else slowing us down. If they wanted to try to get out, they could."

"But…"

"Cy can look after himself." Alex reached out. "Give me your bag."

Eileen sniffed and held out the bag with a shaky hand. Alex took it, then lifted the other two from the floor. With his back against the icy exterior door, he slipped one hand in his pocket to find the keys. Signal lights on the SUV flashed. Snow swirled outside, and strong wind shook the latch. He brushed his elbow close to his side, confirming the weight of the pistol, then pushed against the lock bar and turned to meet the bitter storm.

Alex hung his head as he trudged through the drifting snow. He stopped alongside the rental and set the bags down. With the back door open, he tossed all the bags on the leather seat. Behind the wheel, he searched the controls as he started the engine. The wipers sprang to life, fighting the build-up of snow, and soon cleared enough to give a sufficient view of the world outside. Alex shifted into gear and twisted to look through the back window. He released the brake and pressed down on the accelerator. At first, the SUV hesitated to mount the built-up snow, but it found traction and swerved into the open parking lot.

Alex drove in a wide arc and settled at the apartment entrance. He rolled down the passenger side window. Snow cascaded over the seat and floor. After waving to his mother, he rolled the window up.

Eileen made her way through the door and held her hood closed as she skittered up to the SUV's door. The door handle clicked when she pulled on it.

"Damnit." Alex ran his hand over the controls on the

driver's side door and found the unlock button. Turning back to his mother, he caught a blur of motion. Frantic eyes widened, and her jaw dropped as she was tackled to the ground.

"*Mom.*"

Alex held himself up from his seat, but he could not see his mother or her attacker. After flinging the door wide, he dropped to the ground and wrestled the pistol from his pocket. He slipped and slid as he crested the front of the vehicle. His mother laid screaming as a man straddled her and hammered clenched fists into her face and torso. Dark blood oozed from his sneering lips. His eyes wept redness, and vapor enveloped him.

Alex raised the gun and squeezed the trigger. The attacker twisted as if punched. With one hand over the wound on his chest, he roared through bared teeth, eyes full of hate. He rose up and staggered forward, but the second shot struck his temple. His expression relaxed, and his eyes rolled back as he collapsed into the snow.

Alex rushed to his mother's side and knelt over her. Her breathing shook, and she moaned words without meaning. Blood spray obscured her features, and one eye showed the first signs of swelling. Alex dropped the gun and grabbed his mother's shoulders to sit her up.

Movement at the foyer caught his attention. Amy held the door closed with one hand, and with the other, set the lock. She fixed her eyes on Alex, then turned to retreat into the apparent safety of the lobby.

Alex snarled as he took handfuls of his mother's coat and pulled. "Come on, Mom. *Get up.*"

Thundering footsteps filled the air. Blowing snow obscured figures moving out of the advancing twilight. As they neared, Alex saw the regalia of blood and gore staining their bodies. He searched for the gun, but it slipped from his cold hand. On the third attempt, his fingers squeezed the handle tight. He sighted it as a woman bore down on him with her arms flailing. The barrel discharged, and she spun away, landing next to Alex with a stream of blood spurting from her mouth. Alex scrambled to his feet, firing at anything that moved. He continued to pull the trigger, long after the bullets ran out. The figures kept coming, overrunning the bodies of the fallen.

Alex looked to his mother, prone on the ground and curling in on herself. A groaning figure, with dark hair splayed out, appeared near her. From the veil of snow, another rushed toward Alex. The man's once blue plaid shirt flapped in the wind, now ripped and bloodied. The muscles of his arm and his hands were pock-marked and crusted with a mix of fresh and dry blood. Alex kicked out at the first figure, knocking them to the ground. He feigned, and the plaid man collided with his shoulder. The gun fell, the barrel sizzling as it sank into the snow.

While Alex regained his footing, a woman spun past, straining to grab on to him. She hit the ground, and Alex backed up against the fender of the rental. He drew in a deep breath, then lunged forward and wrapped his mother's arm over his neck. With the passenger door propped open, he lifted her into the seat and slammed the door. Alex bolted around the front of the vehicle with his face wrenched into an unnatural, silent scream. Once behind the wheel, he shifted the SUV into drive and floored the accelerator.

TWENTY-FIVE

An overcast sky held the last of the fading daylight. At the circle, Davie and Francois finished clearing the recent snowfall and arranged everything around the fire. Jacob unzipped his jacket as he helped set food out on the picnic tables. Clint brought down an old propane barbeque and a couple of extra chairs.

The Millers arrived as Jacob removed covers from bowls and trays. Darina was all smiles. Wood bead and banded bracelets jangled on her wrists as she waved to the group. Tight cornrow braids were tied together at her back. The rest of her was bold and colorful, just like her personality. George walked a few steps behind in doubled-up cardigans and khaki pants. He had one arm looped through two aluminum folding chairs. A large tray piled high with buns and sliced bread rested in his hands.

"I just finished some baking before the power went out." Darina motioned to George. "Thought we might as well enjoy it before it goes stale."

Gwen forced a smile. "I'm sure it'll be delicious."

Jacob stepped up to take the tray. George gave him a quick glance, with wide brown eyes, before moving off to set up the chairs.

Clint bounced Hayden on his knee and watched Allena and Parker climb a nearby snowbank. Erica pushed up the sleeves of her sweatshirt and shifted plates along the picnic table as she dished up their dinner. Gwen distributed paper plates and disposable cutlery to the rest of the group while they waited their turn.

Earlier that day, Clint rigged up an oven rack at the fire, allowing them to roast a pan of mixed vegetables and potatoes, and heat a pot of brown beans and foil-wrapped empanadas that Malena pulled from her freezer. Someone brought a green salad and an assorted cheese plate. Davie grilled hot dogs and kielbasa.

When everyone had their fill, Gwen, Malena, and Erica wrapped up the leftovers to be kept. Nicolas made the rounds with a large black garbage bag for what was not. Soon, the group settled around the fire to talk and share stories, or in Francois' case, the odd joke. Gwen brewed a fresh pot of coffee and a batch of hot chocolate for the kids.

The sun set, and shadows danced against the mounds of snow surrounding the circle. Harold sat in a folding chair close to the fire. His white, combed back hair and pale eyes flickered with the firelight. He drank the last of his coffee before setting the mug down on the ground. Slapping his open palms down on the arms of his chair, he leaned forward. "Well, I think that's about it for this old dog." He pushed himself up and adjusted his coat. "Have a good night, everyone."

Penny stood at his side. "I'll see you home, make sure you're all set."

"For pity's sake, the boys brought more wood over this afternoon, and there's food in the house if I need it. You've been fussing over me all day long. I keep telling you, I'll be fine."

"Oh, hush." Penny wrapped an arm around Harold's. "Let's get you home."

Harold scowled and shot Penny a sidelong glance, but followed as she led him up the path to his front door.

Erica sat with both of her boys balanced on her lap. "We should probably head in too." She slid Parker down and took his hand, then lifted and balanced Hayden on her hip. "Allena, honey, finish up your cocoa."

Allena sat in front of Clint cross-legged on the ground with her thin, blonde hair hanging in her face. Her mitted hand carved paths in the snow packed grass. "Aw, Mom…"

"Come on, I'm not messing around. It's time for bed."

Allena scrunched her nose and frowned. Standing, she clapped her hands together to clear the caked-on snow. Erica leaned down and planted a kiss on Clint. "Don't stay out too late."

"I won't."

"Night, everyone."

Gwen waved to them from her chair. "Good night, dear. Sleep well."

Clint waited for the click of his front door closing, then pulled what remained of a six-pack from under his chair. He snapped out a can and set it between his legs. Peeling off the last, he tossed the plastic rings into the fire. "Hey, Frenchie, you want one?"

Francois looked to Rosana. She shrugged and glanced away. "Sure, why not?"

Clint lobbed the can into Francois' waiting hands. He turned to Jacob. "I can run in and grab more if you want one."

"Nah, I'm good. Thanks anyway."

Davie held his hands out from his sides. "Hey, what about me?"

Clint cracked the tab on his can of beer and leaned back to stretch out his legs. "If you want one, you know where they're at."

"Gee, thanks." Davie got to his feet and kicked at a chunk of snow on the ground. At the wood pile, he took a split log in each hand and dropped them onto the fire. Sparks and ash erupted into the air.

Clint waved his hand around his face. "Come on, man. What're you doing?"

"Sorry…" Davie sulked back to the empty picnic table and laid on the long bench.

Jacob watched the embers of the fire. A noise in the distance caught his attention, but he lost it in the crunching snow as Penny returned to the circle. She sat, draping a crocheted blanket over her legs. "Well, that was a nice night."

"It certainly has been, but that doesn't mean it's over." Darina pulled her purse to her lap and took out a small bottle of rum. Emptying her coffee cup onto the ground, she poured herself a generous serving. "Don't be shy now." She passed the bottle to her left.

Gwen smiled. "Don't mind if I do."

The warmth of the fire lulled the group into an easy quiet. Darina hummed to herself, then started singing. It was a gentle tune, soft and flowing. Jacob could not understand the words, but it felt like something a mother would sing to calm her child. He sank back into his chair and half-closed his eyes.

Solid footsteps broke Jacob's trance. It took a moment

before his eyes adjusted to the dim light, and he spotted a figure coming down the road. He set his coffee mug down and focused forward. One figure turned into two, then three, with a fourth lagging behind. Jacob stood, watching the group make their way down the ruts in the snow. The others took notice. Darina's tune trailed off into silence.

Gwen called out. "Good lord, what are you all doing walking around in the middle of the night?"

The group moved in a loose pack with their heads low and arms limp at their sides. Shadows obscured their faces. Any exposed skin steamed like a thoroughbred after a run in the cool morning air.

Francois stepped forward. "Hey guys, everything okay here?"

No response came. Moving from the tire ruts to the path in front of Harold's house, their labored breathing echoed through the crisp night air. When the first figure entered the circle, Darina stepped forward to intercept. "Come on now, don't be rude. Who are you? What are you doing here?"

The stranger walked into range of the light from the fire. The tips of his fingers were worn near to the bone. Blood seeped from the corners of his eyes, nose, and from his slack mouth. It oozed down his chest, soaking into his cotton jacket.

George took a step toward Darina and put a hand on her arm. "Maybe we should—"

The stranger launched forward. Darina raised her arm to protect herself, but the weight of the man toppled them both to the ground. He gnashed his teeth and let loose a choking growl. Darina struggled to push him away. Clint ran up, planted his left foot, and swung the steel tip of his right boot into the stranger's temple. Jacob winced at the sound. It reminded him of eggshells breaking. The stranger went limp and rolled on to his back. George rushed to Darina's side as she sat up. "Oh my…oh my God, are you okay?"

"I'm fine." Darina grabbed George's pantleg to pull herself upright. She held her right arm close to her side. "I need to get home."

Clint stepped in front of them and held his arm out. "Guys, you'd better get back."

Two of the other strangers split ranks and moved around the fire. Jacob searched for something to defend himself with. The axe sat propped beside the wood pile, but he chose a heavy branch instead. He paused in front of Gwen. "Quick, get inside."

Gwen's eyes widened, and her chin trembled. Nicolas backed out of the circle, fighting the urge to run himself. Malena, already home, hid behind their front door. Gwen grabbed Penny's elbow, and they retreated to the far end of the circle. Rosana stopped halfway up the path to her house and waved them over.

Jacob intercepted one of the strangers advancing around the fire. A crown of vapor wrapped around his bald head. Dried blood ran from his shirt collar to the hem hanging down from his protruding belly. His red tinted eyes locked on to Jacob. Closing in, he curled his lip and moaned low.

Jacob stepped back and dug his heels into the snow. "Please, stay where you are."

The man continued to advance with his hands reaching out wide. Jacob arched the branch up into the man's jaw. He stumbled, bits of flesh and bone hanging at odd angles. After steadying himself, he started forward once again. Jacob took two steps back and raised the branch over his head. He brought it down as hard as he could, the impact was felt more than heard. Jacob stepped to one side, and the man collapsed to the ground.

To the right, Clint and Davie stomped and kicked a third man down. The ground, and snow around them, held a crimson hue. On the other side of the fire, toward the main road, a woman stood and watched. Dark gore matted her shoulder-length gray hair against one side of her head. She coughed, and fresh blood sprayed from her lips. She did not move, except for her right hand clenching and unclenching. Jacob's heart pounded hard in his chest, the sensation all he could hear or feel. Davie and Francois moved to either side of the fire. The woman balled her hand into a tight fist and turned her head back to the last figure waiting in the shadows. The woman cocked her head to Davie, then Francois. Backing away, she faded into the distant darkness.

Jacob heaved deep, gulping breaths. He dropped the bloodied branch to the ground. Davie turned to his brother and raised his arms up over his head. "Jesus Christ, Clint, what the hell was that all about?"

"I don't know, man…I just don't know."

Francois held his hands on his waist, and his eyes darted around the circle. "What was wrong with them? The blood, did you see?"

Davie stared at the ground. All color left his face. "What if that shit is contagious, man? What if that happens to us?"

"Shut it, Davie. Nothin's happening to nobody."

Jacob balanced on unsteady legs. He wanted to move, but they refused to respond. Francois came up to him and put a kind hand on his shoulder. "You okay, friend?"

Jacob blinked his eyes. "I think so."

Davie took off his hat and ran his free hand through his hair. "What do we do now?"

"Listen," Clint looked around the circle, "first, we need to get this cleaned up."

"Clint, Jesus, we just killed three people. *We killed them.*"

"Calm the fuck down, Davie. What the hell were we supposed to do? They attacked us. It was self-defense."

Davie paced with the palm of his hand on his forehead. "I don't wanna go to jail, man. I can't do it."

"Christ, Davie, chill out. First the lights and phones, now this? Something big is going down, and I get the feeling we don't know the half of it. Just take a seat and shut up, I need a minute to think." Clint watched the vacant drive and chewed on the dirty nail of his right pointer finger. He looked down to each of the bodies and turned to the waiting group. "Okay, we need some rope and shovels. Garbage bags too."

Jacob lifted a hand. "I've got a couple shovels in the shed."

"Good. Okay. I've got some rope out back." He turned to look at his house. "Stay put a minute though, I need to grab something else first. Davie, come on."

"Jacob?" Gwen stood with one foot on Francois and Rosana's front porch and a hand on the door, ready to close it behind her. Penny and Rosana watched from the front window. "What's going on?"

"I don't know. Stay inside. Keep the door locked."

Gwen's lower lip quivered. She nodded and disappeared behind the door.

Davie returned with his arms wrapped around a length of rope and a box of garbage bags. Clint had two shotguns over his shoulder, both masked in camouflage, including the straps. He held another older looking rifle, looped through his arm and aimed at the ground. Jacob did not know much about guns, but a friend used to keep a few for target practice. He thought it looked like a Russian SKS. Clint dropped two boxes of ammo onto the picnic table.

"Francois, you any good with a rifle?"

"It's been a while, but I'm sure it will come back to me."

Clint slipped the straps of the shotguns down to his hand. "Take one of the Benelli's. Davie, you take the other one. Jacob, can you go see about those shovels now?"

"Sure, I'll be right back."

Clint nodded and turned his attention to Davie and Francois. "Right. So, we'll have to drag these assholes out of here. I'm thinking back to the clearing in the trees."

Francois looked to his front window with the curtains drawn shut. No light or movement showed behind them. "You mean behind my house?"

"Don't worry, we'll get them as far out as we can."

Francois sighed and rubbed at his brow. "Just don't tell Rosana, okay?"

"Hey, she won't hear it from me."

Jacob emerged from the dark with a shovel in each hand, one with a pointed tip and the other square. He also carried a green tarp tucked under his arm. "Figured it might come in handy."

"Good idea." Clint placed the strap of the SKS over his shoulder. "Okay, Davie—"

A series of sharp pops sounded from the south, four in a row. A short pause, then another. Clint squinted into the night.

Davie's voice came quiet, "Clint? What was that?"

"What the hell do ya think it was? Grab the rope. We need to clean this up and get inside, like right fuckin' now."

TWENTY-SIX

The road out of the area had been traveled enough to make it passable. Alex took a wrong turn early on and brought them south on 219, instead of east as he wanted. Soon, they caught up with others fleeing the area. The road narrowed to two lanes, and they continued in a tight convoy. Alex considered pulling over to find a place to stop, but he also thought about the potential safety that came with numbers.

A glow rose on the horizon. At first, Alex wondered if it might be the rising sun. Soon, the pinpoint of light grew to an oasis. A city, it seemed, but he was not sure which one or if they might have crossed the state line into Pennsylvania. Shadowy structures came into view. Abandoned vehicles, concrete barriers, and barbed wire littered the road. His phone began to bing and buzz in the cupholder. Alex unplugged the charger cord and set the lit phone on his lap.

The display scrolled as notifications piled up. One message in particular stood out. Dividing his attention between the road and his phone, he ran a thumb along the edge of the screen. A text from Ivy. Alex cleared the tightness in his throat and set the phone down on its face. He put both hands on the wheel and pulled into the queue.

An older sedan passed the barricade, and a lone soldier stepped forward to halt them with one hand out. In addition to the standard uniform, the checkpoint guard donned doubled-up nitrile gloves and a cotton bandanna tied over his nose and mouth. His rifle pointed at the ground with a finger hovering over the trigger. He stood well back from the vehicle, eyes darting across and around it.

When the driver's door opened, the soldier hurried forward and kicked it shut. Shouting, he raised his rifle. The brake lights on the car went dark, and the engine revved. Without hesitation, the soldier squeezed the trigger. Sharp flashes of muzzle fire lit his face. Lurching forward, the car veered away from the crossing before settling in the deep snow. Soldiers flooded in from the shadows and surrounded the car. They opened the doors and pulled bodies to the ground.

Alex shifted the SUV into gear, cranked the wheel hard to the left, and pressed his foot to the floor. He fought to move in a straight line as he accelerated north and away from the light.

Eileen stirred in her seat. Her good eye fluttered, and she moaned. Alex eased off the accelerator and lifted an open bottle of water from the console. He put it in his mother's unsteady hand. She gripped it and raised it to her lips. After swallowing, she held it in her lap. "Where…where are we?"

"On the road. Don't worry, I'm going to find a safe place to stop."

Eileen's head bobbed once before she lowered it to her shoulder and closed her eyes.

———

Alex continued north to West Seneca. The strain of keeping the compact SUV on the road, and away from the worst of the chaos, wore on him. The world around them continued to burn. Streets remained empty, save for the people being chased, or those doing the chasing. Opportunities to find a safe haven seemed more distant than ever. Alex covered his mouth with his forearm and yawned wide. He slowed the SUV until it bogged down in the snow.

From the west, the Peace Bridge loomed a black silhouette over the river. Deserted vehicles and smoldering debris littered the crossing, but a scant path remained. The bridge looked quiet as well. Alex did not think too hard on it. He simply drove on, at times, in the opposite lane to shorten the journey. He navigated around scorched vehicles and bodies until they were past the American crossing and over the bridge.

Two blocks past the Canadian border, he pulled into a lot with several vehicles parked at odd angles. Alex backed into a dark corner, allowing a clear line to the open road, and turned the engine off. His mother slept, pressed up against the door. He searched for the adjustment on his seat, reclined, and closed his eyes.

———

Alex flinched as a cry rang out from the street in front of them. Two women ran down the ruts in the road. Unrelenting snow made it hard to see, but it looked like they had been in some sort of fight. One had streaks of blood on her face. The other pressed her hand against a dark stain on her leg and ran with a limp.

The side street to the west erupted with sound and light. A

late model Subaru, decked out as a rally car, roared around the corner at speed. Its four-cylinder engine howled into the night. Behind it, a white rooster tail fanned as it drifted through the deep snow. It straightened out and accelerated toward the pair. When it made contact, it drew one woman under the wheels. The other pitched to the side just in time. The car fishtailed but regained its line and sped off to be obscured by the storm.

The woman thrown to the side of the road sat propped up on one arm, crying out and inching toward her friend. The woman in the middle of the road laid twisted and powdered with snow. Alex noticed movement, albeit slight.

Multiple figures stormed out of the surrounding darkness. They stumbled and overran each other, shrouded in a fine haze. The woman on the side of the road was swarmed first, her defenses ineffective against the kicking, biting, and scratching. Once her screams subsided, the mob lost interest. As they dispersed, one stopped at the woman in the middle of the street. After watching her a moment, they moved off with the others.

"Alex?"

Alex darted a glance at his mother. "Yeah, Mom?"

"What's happening?"

"Nothing" He pulled the blanket around his mother's neck and rested the back of his hand on her forehead. He moved it to the other side to confirm. "You feeling all right?"

She attempted a smile. "Like I've been run over by a bus."

Alex sighed. He took two liquid ibuprofen capsules from an unmarked bottle in the console and held them out with a bottle of water. "Here, time for a couple more."

Eileen shook her head and turned to the side window.

"Come on."

She tilted her head back and looked at Alex from the

corner of her eye. Nudging her with his elbow, he pushed the pills in front of her face. She raised a shaky hand, brought them to her mouth, and slid them past her lips. After sipping from the bottle, she handed it back to Alex, then adjusted the blanket lower on her lap and sank into the seat.

Alex watched her breathe, shallow and strained. He looked at the open bottle, then tightened the cap and set it in the cup holder. Behind his seat, he reached for a fresh bottle and held it as he watched the snow fall through the windshield.

TWENTY-SEVEN

Jacob stared at the ceiling. Dull light from the emerging sun showed his breath rising in the still air. The generator ran dry sometime in the middle of the night. Checking the fuel level had diminished to a forgotten priority. Restful sleep eluded him as images of blood and violence returned fresh every time he closed his eyes.

Jacob slipped on his coat as he hobbled toward the kitchen. He took an empty glass from behind the sink and held it under the faucet. Lifting the handle, a trickle of water came out, but it soon tapered to nothing. He sighed. "Great."

He set the empty glass in the sink and parted the kitchen curtains. Harold sat at a picnic table with Penny and Gwen. Clint warmed his hands at the fire, his rifle strung over his shoulder, and Francois and Nicolas chatted off to the right. Davie headed up the path toward Clint and Erica's house. When his breath fogged up the window to the point he could not see through, Jacob pushed back from the counter and went out to join his neighbors.

Smoke hung thick in the air. It held a tinge that made it

clear it was more than the group's usual campfire. With the ground scraped clean and fresh snow shoveled in, he had to look closely for signs of the struggle.

Harold nodded at Jacob as he approached. Jacob sat facing out at the end of the picnic table. Penny and Gwen each flashed a tight, unhappy smile.

"Morning, dear."

"Morning. Is everyone's water out?"

"I'm afraid so. We've made a plan to start hauling clean snow and filling bathtubs. Hopefully, the pipes don't freeze up. We can still flush toilets for now. Francois said he has a stack of buckets we can use. We'll figure it out."

"Okay. What else is going on?"

Gwen turned a mug of coffee in her hands. "Just trying to make sense of it all, I guess."

Penny pointed her chin toward Clint, Nicolas, and Francois. "The boys said they found tracks all over the place. No signs of anyone still around, though."

"Francois went to check on the Millers a little while ago. George got mad and told him they were fine and to leave them alone."

Clint walked up to the table and dropped a stack of wallets. "They were from Buffalo, all three of 'em."

Jacob bent to rest his elbows on his knees. "You think that means anything?"

"Not sure yet."

"Penny mentioned you found tracks?"

Clint pulled at his ear and glanced behind him to the abandoned house. "Yeah, a few. It looks like someone was trying to get inside a couple places."

"What?"

"Yeah. The door at the empty place took a couple good

hits, but it held. Someone was at Harold's and around George's place, too."

"Pardon me?" Gwen set the flat of her hand on her knee and leaned forward. "You didn't mention anything about that earlier."

Clint's eyes darted between Gwen and the fire. "Sorry, I didn't want everyone freaking out."

"We need to know these things, Clint, for everyone's sake."

Clint scratched at the back of his neck. "You're right, it won't happen again."

Francois and Nicolas took positions on either side of the table. Nicolas tucked his hands in his pockets and moved foot-to-foot. Francois kept his focus on the road in with a shotgun at this back.

Shaking his smokes free from his breast pocket, Clint lit a cigarette. "All right, we need to make sure we've got everything straight. It's been, what, two days now? For the sake of sharing, has anyone seen anything? People, vehicles, anything out of the ordinary? I was just thinking, I haven't heard an airplane since this whole thing started."

Francois pivoted to face the group. "Well, they did shut down airspace because of the storm. I think I heard a helicopter early this morning. Along the river, to the east."

Nicolas adjusted his glasses. "That's something at least, isn't it? You would think that the police, or even the army, would be out searching. If the blackout is large enough that we can't see lights in Buffalo, or at the falls, it has to be a big deal."

"We have to assume that we're gonna get hit again. Next time, we need to be better prepared." Clint pointed his finger to the road in. "I think we need to look into setting up some sort of barricade. The snow is pretty deep in most places, but it thins out where the tree cover is heaviest."

Harold lifted a trembling hand. "We need to do something about the tire tracks. Led them right in as far as I can see."

Clint's face turned red. "Yeah, well, they're coming in from everywhere, but we'll figure something out."

Jacob squeezed his gloved hands tight. "What are the chances we can get another vehicle out to block the road in?"

Clint scratched at the stubble on his chin. "I don't know, man. We've cleared a fair bit out, but it's still gotta be too deep. Plus, I don't think that would do much good if they're all on foot."

Gwen warmed her hands around the coffee cup in front of her. "I'm sure we can come up with something."

"Okay, well, everyone think on it." Clint walked back to the fire. "What about weapons? I don't mind offering up the guns, but this is all I've got. Erica made me get rid of most of them after the kids were born."

The group looked back and forth to each other. Harold held a gruff expression on his face and stayed silent. Gwen shrunk her chin to her chest and raised her hand to shoulder height, wiggling her fingers.

Clint raised an eyebrow. "You been holding out on me, Gwen?"

"I kept my dad's old rifle, for sentimental reasons more than anything else. It's just a little twenty-two."

"Oh…" Clint dropped his shoulders.

"Well, I've got my .357 too."

Francois stifled a cough. "You…you have a Magnum?"

Gwen lifted her nose. "I do. It's registered and everything. I go to the range every year on my birthday."

Clint snickered. "That's awesome."

"Now, listen. I know the rules, and you can't just go shooting it off wherever you like."

"Gwen, do me a favor, and look at what's going on here. Even if the police do come around, I think they have more important things to worry about."

Nicolas held out a low hand. "Come on now, Clint, let's calm down a little."

Gwen placed her overlapped hands on her lap. "No, it's okay, Nicolas. Clint is right. I'll get it ready when I head in next."

"Great. Anyone else?" Clint looked around to shrugging shoulders and sheepish expressions. "I'll take that as a no."

Arms flailing, Davie sprinted into the circle with his mouth slack and his face drained of color.

"What the hell are you doing, Davie?"

"There's a…someone…under the…"

Harold straightened. "Take a breath, son."

Davie pitched forward and put his hands on his knees. After two deep breaths, he raised up. "One of those freaks is, like, *sleeping* under my camper."

"Come on, Davie, really?"

Davie pointed back the way he came. "It's under my goddamned camper, Clint. Go look for yourself if you don't believe me."

Clint eyed Davie as he slipped the SKS off his shoulder. "Stay here." He waved at Francois to follow and moved up the path.

Around the back corner of the house, they approached with their guns raised and each step carefully placed. Stacks of sagging boxes, rusting barrels, and various car parts surrounded Davie's camper. A single, uneven path led to his door, the only disturbance in the otherwise pristine snow cover. Clint paused and noticed tiny flecks of red along their route. He held out a hand for Francois to stay put while he moved to the back of the camper.

At the left side, Clint stuck a boot out and flicked a crumpled tarp out of the way. He dropped to one knee and looked up the side of the camper. He only saw trash. Standing, he moved to the right. A faint wisp of steam drifted out from under the overhang. He stepped back and pointed. Francois crept to his side, shotgun at the ready.

Clint kept his voice low. "Cover me?"

With a quick nod from Francois, Clint knelt beside the camper. In the shadows, a figure curled up on the ground, with the snow around them stained red. Clint heard the shallow rattle of strained breathing, and he could see the rapid rise and fall of their chest.

Clint reached out with his rifle until the muzzle made contact, pushed forward twice, then jumped back. The figure moaned and adjusted their position. Clint waited, but they remained still. He looked back to Francois, who shrugged. Clint bent down for another look. When his eyes adjusted, he saw a face. A young man's face. Blood trickled down from a half-open eye. The shredded flesh on his cheek exposed crimson teeth underneath. His torn and stained clothing masked his form. Without shoes, the bottoms of his feet swelled, purple and raw.

Clint motioned Francois over. "Check it out."

Francois knelt beside Clint. "Sleeping?"

"Deep sleep. Poked him, and he barely moved."

"Smells pretty bad."

"Yeah it does."

Francois pressed at his temple. "So, what now?"

"I only see one option."

"You sure?"

"Pretty sure."

Francois laid the Benelli across his legs. "I mean, what if we can help him or something?"

"Come on, man. Does that look like someone who can be helped?"

Francois looked away. "No, I guess not."

Eyeing the figure, Clint ran a hand through his messy hair. "Shit."

The young man's eyes opened. He blinked and focused on Clint and Francois. Upper lip raised, he let out a low growl. His arms extended to pull his body upright.

"Son of a..." Clint raised the SKS and squeezed the trigger.

Francois fell back, covering his ears. The figure under the camper went limp.

Clint scrambled to his feet. "*Goddamn it.*" He drilled his heel into the ground with each syllable. Slipping the rifle strap over his shoulder, he stormed off.

Back at the fire, the group watched as Clint marched down the path. "Davie, it's your camper, go clean it up." He snatched a shovel on his way through the circle. "Jacob, grab some gear and a shotgun. We need to go check on the Bensons."

———

Jacob stopped to grab a few things from the house and ran to catch up to Clint. While he was not clear as to what 'gear' entailed, Jacob filled his backpack with a couple bottles of water and a small assortment of hand tools. On his way through the circle, he took the shotgun from Davie and a handful of ammunition from the box on the picnic table.

Out in the open, they were able to see fires burning in town. Smoke rose in jagged pillars and connected the sky to the ground. Things appeared worse across the river. Flashes and pops broke through the foul haze but not much else. They saw no sign of the police or fire department.

Jacob and Clint stood in the road, facing the long driveway to the Benson's property. Ruts left by Clint's truck had been trampled flat, and they held a blotchy pink hue. Away from the road, footsteps followed the treeline where drifting left thin snow cover.

At the top of the driveway, an older two-story stood off to the right. The front steps were clear, save for a light dusting that worked its way around the porch overhang. Jacob saw no movement or smoke from the chimney. Parked out front, a newer sedan remained half-blanketed in snow. A double-wide mobile home sat across the lot. Tracks showed around the house, but it seemed otherwise left alone. A larger garage stood at the top of the drive. A workshop and a few smaller outbuildings were nestled further back in the trees.

Clint checked both ways up the road and lifted the cigarette from his lips. "Well, you ready?"

Jacob swallowed to clear his throat, then fussed with the strap on his pack. "Guess so."

"All right, let's do this then."

Clint flicked the cigarette butt into the snow and pushed the SKS back on his shoulder. He adjusted his grip on the shovel and hacked at the snow in wide, sweeping motions. Jacob stayed a few feet behind, shielding his face from the surge. When Clint pushed through to the already cleared section of the driveway, he dropped the shovel and bent forward, resting his hands on his knees.

Jacob came up beside him. "You okay?"

"Yeah, just need to catch my breath."

Dense cloud cover held the sun at bay. Chilled wind blew in from the north. Jacob kept an eye on the trees around them. A group of birds made soft noises in the distance.

Clint stood upright and adjusted the rifle strap, then led the way to the two-story house. He climbed up the front steps while Jacob waited at the crest of the driveway. Rapping his knuckles on the front door, he stepped back. No answer. Clint looked to Jacob. His cheeks puffed out as he exhaled. "Damnit."

Clint reached out for the doorknob. It turned, and the latch released with the sound of a rusty spring stretching. Clint pushed the door open and leaned inside. "Andrew? Cassandra?"

He did not hear a response.

"Mrs. Benson? Hello?"

Clint stared at the frosted door sill. "Shit. Just shit." Shrugging the rifle down his arm, he grabbed the forestock. He kicked the steel toes of his boots against the door frame and stepped into the house. "Come on, let's check it out."

Clint raised the SKS level to his shoulder. The wood subfloor creaked with each step as he moved up the stairs of the entryway and through the living room. "Hello? It's Clint from across the road."

Jacob stayed behind as Clint went around a corner and into the kitchen. He noticed a hint of smoke in the air, but it did not feel much warmer than outside. Clint returned a few seconds later. "Nothing. Saw stairs back that way."

Jacob followed Clint up a narrow, wood-paneled hallway. He paused at a plain door near the end.

"You know what basements are like in these old houses, right? They smell funny and have all sorts of weird hidden spots. I used to have nightmares about being trapped in an old dirt basement. I'm just saying, if you feel the need to check it out, then be my guest. I sure as shit ain't goin' down there."

Jacob stared at the closed door. "I'm good."

"Right. Upstairs it is then."

Clint moved to the end of the hall. He sighted the rifle up and around the corner. "Hello? Anyone home?" He inched up the stairs with his back sliding against the wall, not waiting for a response.

Clint checked the first of the three doors on the upper level. Sparsely decorated, a few certificates in plain plastic frames hung on the wall. A large desk occupied the far wall. Stacks of notebooks and a mess of papers scattered across the top. A steel four-drawer filing cabinet sat beside it. The room otherwise sat empty.

Jacob went into the next. A king size bed took up most of the space. A pair of matching tall and low dressers lined opposite walls. He kicked at a dirty sock on the floor and backed out of the room. Jacob and Clint stared down the hall to the third and final door.

"So, uh, it's your turn, right?"

Jacob turned and cocked an eyebrow. "What?"

"It's your turn, man. Go on, open the door."

"But I just did the last room."

"Yeah, but I was the first one in the house, and I checked the kitchen and the other bedroom. You get this one. Congratulations."

Jacob rolled his eyes and sighed. "Okay, whatever."

He pushed past Clint and positioned himself in front of the door. Knocking twice, he leaned in to listen. Receiving no response, he wrapped his fingers around the brass knob and turned it. Jacob winced at the harsh groan of the hinges. Shotgun raised, he stepped in and scanned the largest of the three rooms.

Next to the open door sat a small bed with a wrought iron frame. Along the adjacent wall, two windows with the curtains drawn tight. At the end of the room, a compact brick hearth fireplace. A pile of ashes and half-burned logs sat inside, but the fire had been out for some time. In the corner by the fireplace, a brown corduroy recliner heaped with blankets rested next to a round side table. A crossword book laid face down on top with an empty glass beside it. Tucked behind the table, a tall floor lamp stood with a patterned plastic shade.

"It's clear. Come on in."

Clint stopped beside Jacob, watching the brown recliner. "You sure about that?"

"What do you mean?" Jacob squinted at the mound on the chair. A light-colored comforter, with a vintage floral pattern, covered most of it. Near the top, a face showed through a fold in a black and orange crocheted blanket. Pale, wrinkled skin surrounded a petite nose and tight, thin lips.

"I think that's Mrs. Benson. I mean, Andrew's mom. It's Deborah."

"Shit."

"Yeah."

"Do you think, I mean, is she…"

"I don't know, man."

"What should we do?"

"What do you mean, what should we do? If she's dead, we're leaving her ass here."

"I don't know if I can do that."

"What do you propose, then? Drag her out? Then what? I'm not saying I'm overly fond of her, but I sure as hell ain't dumping her with those other freaks. She's just fine where she is until we can get some help."

"I guess you're right. Shouldn't we, you know, check her out to be sure?"

Clint took a knee and set his rifle on the floor. He lifted his ballcap and ran his free hand through his hair. "Like this day couldn't get any fuckin' weirder." He reached toward the pile of blankets but hesitated. He flexed his fingers. "Damnit." Clint put his hand on the blankets and shook them side to side. "Mrs. Benson? Deborah?"

Clint paused, then twisted back to Jacob. "Doesn't look like—"

The blankets moved, and Deborah's hand came up to cover her mouth with a crumpled tissue. A choking cough echoed through the quiet room. Clint flung both arms over his head and rolled over onto the floor. "*Jesus Christ.*"

Jacob crouched down in front of the chair and set the shotgun at his feet. "Mrs. Benson, are you all right?"

Deborah's eyes fluttered open, but her lids stayed low. She spoke with a weak, raspy tone. "Who…who are you? Where's Andrew and Cassie?"

"My name is Jacob. Do you remember Gordon and Delia from across the way? I'm their grandson." Jacob pointed to Clint, laying spread eagle on the floor. "That's Clint."

Clint raised his head and let out a loud exhale. "I swear to Christ, man, I nearly shit my pants."

Deborah wiped the corner of her mouth with the tissue. "Where's Andrew?"

"We're not sure. When did you see him last?"

"He was worried about the power. He said they were going to get help, but I should stay here."

"Do you remember when they left?"

"I'm not sure." She pulled her hand back under the blanket. "I'm so thirsty. Can you get me a glass of water?"

"Yeah, sure." Jacob flipped his backpack to the floor, unzipped the top, and pulled out a bottle of water. After unscrewing the cap, he picked up the empty glass from the side table and filled it halfway. "Here you go."

Deborah brought both hands out from under the blankets and gripped the glass near the base. She slurped down most of the water and held it out for Jacob to take back. "Thank you."

"Clint, we have to get her out of here."

Pacing, Clint stared at the ceiling. "Yeah, I guess we do."

"Mrs. Benson, do you think you can stand? We're going to take you back across the way. We'll get you warmed up and have something to eat. Does that sound good?"

"But, what about Andrew and Cassie?"

"Don't worry, we'll leave them a note. Is there anything we need to bring?"

"My pills. They're in the bathroom." Her hand searched, patting around under the blankets. "I have my inhaler in my pocket."

"Okay, that's it? Are you sure?"

"Yes."

"Good. Can you stand?"

She nodded.

"All right, let's get you up, and we'll get out of here."

TWENTY-EIGHT

Alex opened the hatch and dropped an armload of loose items inside. Scrap fence board, branches, and a metal pipe stacked tight against the wall of bags and totes puzzle-pieced in the back.

Pulling a multi-tool from the pocket of his jacket, he popped the panels at the back corner of the SUV open, unhooked the light assemblies, and twisted the bulbs out. Following the line, he cut the exposed wire from the third brake light.

"Alex?"

"Yeah, Mom?"

"I'm hungry."

"Almost done. Hold on."

From a small foam cooler, he removed two stainless cylinders and a clear bag of tablets. With a tab in each cylinder, he packed them with clean snow, then closed the hatch and strode up the left side of the vehicle. Leaning inside the driver's door, he released the hood. He set the full cylinders against the engine, away from any moving parts, and extracted two now melted cannisters, standing them beside the hood latch. Reaching down, he twisted the retaining rings from the headlight bulbs, took them from their connectors, and slid them in his pocket. Back behind the wheel, the engine revved to life, and he adjusted the heat controls.

Eileen gave a weak cough. "When are we going to be there?"

"I don't know. Soon, I hope."

Her eyes fluttered. "Don't forget to call your mother, Boyd."

"What?" Alex raised an eyebrow, searching for the memory of when he last heard his father's name.

"We always call to let her know we're home safe. I don't want her to worry."

Alex watched his mother. Her head bobbed as she fought to remain conscious. Her skin lacked proper color, and perspiration beaded on her upper lip.

He turned away and rubbed his dry eyes. "Sure, I'll let her know. Don't worry."

Eileen pushed the blanket from her lap to the floor and unzipped her coat. "Thank you." Her voice trailed away, and her head tilted to the window as she closed her eyes.

TWENTY-NINE

Jacob brought Deborah a peanut butter and jam sandwich, and another glass of water, before helping her downstairs. She stopped for a bathroom break, then dressed for the journey.

Deborah felt well enough to walk most of the way, with help from Jacob and Clint through the deeper sections. Their pace was slow, but in the end, they managed to get back to the community without incident.

Jacob came to the circle after dropping his supplies at home. Francois sat in a lawn chair near the fire with one of the Benelli's across his lap. Davie milled about, keeping a watchful eye on the road in. Jacob walked up beside Francois with his hands in the pockets of his jacket.

"Hello, friend."

"Hey, Francois."

"Quite a morning."

"Yes, it was."

"Are you all right?"

"Yeah, just tired."

Francois nodded.

"Where'd Clint get off to?"

"Oh," Francois turned in his chair and motioned to the back of the circle, "he went to check on Erica and the little ones. Said he'd be back soon."

"Okay. You guys see anything while we were away?"

"No, nothing new. We were out in the trees earlier, cutting some down to build a barricade of sorts, but we didn't see anything out of the ordinary. Considering the circumstances, at least."

"Yeah, us neither. It's strange, right? You think maybe it's over?"

Francois shrugged. "I'm not sure."

Jacob took a step toward the fire, held out a hand, and watched Davie pace. They both turned at the sound of boot steps in the snow. Nicolas walked toward the fire, his long coat and looped scarf stirring in the breeze.

"I saw you were back. Earlier, I mean. I wanted to give everyone time to warm up. How did your adventure go?"

"All right. There were tracks and stuff, but no sign of any more of those…you know. Mrs. Benson said Andrew and Cassandra went out to find help, but we have no idea when they left or where they are. We brought Mrs. Benson back with us."

"I saw. Is she okay?"

"I'm sure she will be." Jacob tilted his head to Gwen and Penny's front door. "She's still getting settled, though.

"That's good."

"Yeah."

"How was everything here?"

Nicolas shrugged. "Quiet, for the most part."

"Good."

Nicolas agreed.

Jacob looked to the sound of an opening door. Gwen stepped out onto her porch with a large pot of slush water in her hands. Sensing she was being watched, she gave Jacob a thin smile and shimmied down the path to the fire.

"Gentlemen."

"Hey, Gwen."

Nicolas adjusted his glasses. "How is Mrs. Benson?"

"Oh, she's fine." Gwen smiled. "Tough old bird, that one. Just a little dehydrated."

"Good to hear."

Gwen balanced the pot on the fire. She patted Jacob's arm as she set off back to her house. "You boys did good."

"Thanks, Gwen."

"We're getting some dinner started, be back soon."

Francois smiled wide. "Best news I've heard in a while."

Gwen snickered to herself and waved a hand as she walked away.

————

Jacob tossed a stack of used paper plates onto the fire. Gwen placed a cover on a pot full of scraps. "If we're all done here, I'll head in and check on everyone." She lifted the pot. "Plus, I'm sure the cats are hungry."

"Sure, see you in a bit."

Clint flicked the butt end of his cigarette into the fire and cracked a fresh beer. He looked up to the sun as it neared the horizon. "It'll be dark soon. We should get ready."

Francois settled his hands into his pockets. "What do you have in mind?"

"I'm thinking me and Davie should take first shift."

Penny frowned. "Are you sure? You've had a pretty busy day already."

"It's okay. I took a nap, I'll be fine. Who wants to take over in the morning?"

Jacob raised his hand. "I can."

Nicolas stepped forward. "I'll join you."

"Well then," Francois leaned over in his chair and grabbed a cold can from the snow, "since I don't need to be up early…" He smiled and cracked the tab.

"Cool. You guys need a wake-up call, or can you set an alarm?"

Nicolas frowned. "I'm afraid our phones are dead, and I believe everything else we have in the house needs electricity."

Jacob looked toward his front door. "I've got an old wind-up clock, I think. Nicolas, I can come and grab you in the morning."

"Excellent. Six work for you guys?"

"Sure."

"Okay, we're set. Francois, you got this for a bit? I'm gonna say good night to the kids."

Francois gave a thumbs-up and slurped from his tipped beer.

Clint pointed to Nicolas and Jacob as he started toward his house. "You two rest up. See you in the morning."

"Have a good night, Clint."

———

Gun shots woke Jacob in the night. His heart raced as he jumped out of bed and ran to his front porch.

Clint and Davie positioned themselves on each side of the

fire and shot into the darkness. Jacob rubbed the sleep from his eyes and focused up the road. Three figures moved down the ruts. A man, in a long bathrobe and threadbare boxer shorts, limped hard after a shot struck his thigh. Behind him, a heavy-set woman in a baggy dress had one forearm hanging by a cord of skin and muscle. The brothers stopped to reload as round-after-round was spent. It seemed to Jacob they were only making a mess of things.

Jacob watched as a bullet ripped through the knee of a tall, skinny man with a shaved head. He folded to the ground like a pile of sticks, but turned over, and started crawling toward the brothers. Eyes bulging and teeth bared, he spit blood with every irregular breath.

"Hold up, hold up, I got this." Clint sighted his rifle and pulled the trigger. The man's head split open like a firework, and his body slumped flat against the ground.

Eyes wide, Davie pointed up the road. "Did you see that—"

A sharp crack came from their left. The man in the bathrobe fell face forward into the snow. A click, another crack, and the heavy woman crumpled to the ground.

Harold stood on his porch, the barrel of his rifle still smoking. Hand on the railing, he leaned forward, staring Clint and Davie down with a scowl. Without saying a word, he pivoted on his heel and shuffled back into his house.

"You boys going to clean up your mess now?"

Clint and Davie both jumped. Gwen hovered in her doorway, holding her sweater tight to her body.

"Jesus, Gwen, you scared me half to death."

Gwen frowned and held her ground.

Clint tapped Davie on the chest with the back of his hand. "Come on, let's go before more show up."

Jacob gave Gwen a quick wave before she headed back inside. He watched the brothers drag the first of the bodies away and decided to leave them to it. He made his way back to bed and crawled under the blankets.

Sleep did not come easy. He woke a few hours later, thinking he heard more shooting. Jacob rolled over and waited, but all remained quiet. Clint and Davie appeared to have learned their lesson.

It seemed like moments later that his room filled with the sound of ringing. Jacob peeled his eyes open as the alarm slowed and stopped. He rubbed at his face with his palm and exhaled. "Damnit."

THIRTY

Jacob trudged down his porch steps and past his truck. Dawn would soon give way to the rising sun. Snow, disturbed by the chaos of the night before, held a dark tinge. At the end of his driveway, he stopped, looked up, and held his hand out flat. Falling flakes settled on his palm. Running a finger over it, he realized it was ash, not snow.

Wearing a faded USO ballcap, Harold sat in one of the lawn chairs by the fire. A camping blanket covered his shoulders, and his rifle stood propped by his side. Gwen knelt at the fire, adding fresh wood. "Morning, dear."

"Morning, Gwen. Morning, Harold. Where are Clint and Davie?"

"We've already sent the little boys off to bed." Gwen pulled a towel from her shoulder and held it out to Jacob, then motioned to a sauce pot sitting at the edge of the fire. "Here, take this, and go wash up."

"Thanks. I'll be quick."

"Take your time, dear. Breakfast should be ready when you get back."

Jacob lowered the pot down beside the kitchen sink. Unzipping his coat, he shrugged it onto the counter, then peeled off his sweater and t-shirt and let them drop to the floor. He kept watch through the thin break in the curtains as he washed.

With the pot in the sink, he leaned over, splashing handfuls of water down his hair and face, and worked it into his coarse beard. Jacob spread his arms and planted his hands flat on the counter. With his face down, he let the water drip into the sink. He stayed until he could not take the cold any longer, then scurried to his bedroom to dry off and find a fresh shirt. Back in the kitchen, he pulled his sweater and jacket on. He left for the circle with the pot gripped in one hand.

"Good timing, breakfast is ready to go." Gwen tugged her jacket tight around her. "Now, it's my turn for a wash."

"Thanks, Gwen. I really appreciate it."

"No problem, dear. Be back shortly." Humming to herself, Gwen shuffled up the path and her porch steps. Just before the door, she stopped. "I forgot to mention," she motioned to the back of the circle, "Nicolas was out earlier. Said he was going to have a bite to eat with the wife, then he'll be back."

Jacob waved in acknowledgment.

Gwen pulled her front door open, pot of water balanced in one hand, and went inside.

Jacob picked a plate off the seat of the chair beside Harold and sat down. He poked at the plate with his fork. "Beans? For breakfast?"

"It's an English thing. Think Gwen's trying to expand our horizons." Harold shrugged. "It's hot, and I didn't have to cook. So, there's that."

Jacob thought it strange, but his stomach told him not

strange enough to complain about. He polished off his plate of beans, sausage, and bread in a minute flat.

Jacob motioned to the growing pile of wallets and identification on the picnic table. "What's the count?"

"Five more from across the border. Got the first from our side. The boys said there were more, but they didn't come close enough to need dealing with."

Jacob picked the hull of a bean from between his teeth. "Not good. Clint and Davie must have calmed down after the first few."

Harold scowled. "Stupid kids. I'm not sure what's going on exactly, but I don't think those two are taking it serious enough by half. If you're smart, some things you only need to learn once. Second time, you might be dead."

"I'm not trying to make light of the situation or anything, but it's a good thing you were around."

Harold gave a stiff nod. He wrapped his hand around the barrel of his rifle and leaned it into the firelight. "Was my dad's. Remington 308. I learned to shoot on it as a kid. Never thought I'd have to use those skills on another human being, though. Wasn't a fan when I had to do it during the war, and my opinion hasn't changed much since." His face softened, pausing to stare at his arthritic and bent hands. "I never would've thought I'd be sitting here with it so many years later. At the time, I was happy to get back home, especially after I met Martha. I was a big fish in a little pond. They called me a hero, even though I could barely function out in the world."

Jacob put his fidgeting hands on his lap and watched the fire. "I can't imagine that was easy."

"Well, a lot has changed since then. I'm only glad she isn't around to see all this nonsense."

"I'm sorry, I didn't mean to…"

"Don't be sorry, son. We had a good life together. That's all that needs to be said."

"Fair enough." Jacob tossed his paper plate into the fire and left his fork on the nearest picnic table. Scanning the community, he spotted movement among the trees behind the Miller's house. Rising up, Jacob saw George stumble in the snow, pulling a garden wagon full of broken timber.

Jacob settled back. "You see that?"

Harold turned. "Old Georgie-boy is out every morning about this time. Thinks he's being sneaky, but I've seen him. Seen other things too. Lights and such. Those two have more secrets than we know about, that's for sure."

"You didn't mention it to anyone else?"

"None of my damn business. Fool wants to make a go of it on his own, then let him. Those two have been weird from the start. No skin off my behind."

"I suppose so."

Francois and Rosana pulled camp chairs to the circle and joined the fire. Gwen returned soon after with a towel still wrapped around her head.

Rosana lifted a hand from her pocket and wiggled her fingers. "Good morning, everyone."

Harold adjusted his position and nodded. "Nice to see you out."

Rosana gave a shy smile and shrugged. "Well, with everything going on, I felt it best to stay inside." She interlocked her fingers with Francois'. "But, since I have been told I will be safe, I thought it was time to get some fresh air."

Francois kissed her hand. "I won't let anything happen to you, my love."

"The boys said they didn't see anything after five or so.

I've been out here since just before six, and I haven't seen anything either." Harold looked to Jacob. "None of those things, anyway."

"Well, let's hope it stays that way."

Harold huffed and looked to his front door. "If it's all right with you all, I'm going to head in for a bit." He motioned toward Rosana and Francois. "Breakfast is keeping warm on the grill, help yourselves."

Francois patted his stomach. "Sounds good, I'm starving."

Harold looped the rifle strap over his shoulder and walked away with a short right step. He stopped at the edge of the circle and raised a finger. "Oh, Jacob, I forgot to mention, Clint said to say that he'd be out around eleven. He wants to make another trip and asked for you to get a few things together."

Harold pulled a folded piece of paper from his pocket. Jacob walked over to take it from him.

"Did he say where he wants to go?"

"He didn't, just that he has a plan."

Jacob unfolded the note and surveyed the words scratched in blue pencil crayon. His eyebrows pinched together as he scanned the list of items. "Okay, I'll be ready."

Harold turned to walk home. "Good luck."

———

The list rested open on the kitchen table with a checkmark by each item. On the chair beside him, Jacob positioned his backpack with the top spread wide. He lined the main compartment with a handful of big green garbage bags, then added two bottles of water, and two peanut butter and strawberry jam sandwiches, made with the last of his bread.

He stashed a pair of wire cutters, a box cutter, and a couple screwdrivers in a side pocket. Tucked in the other, two sharpened pencils and a map he found hiding in the back of the kitchen junk drawer. It was almost ten years old, but Jacob assumed the area had not changed much since then. Topping everything off with a spare sweater and an extra pair of socks, he zipped the pack closed and lifted a strap over his shoulder.

Gwen waved Jacob over as he returned to the circle. She pointed to one of the picnic tables. A bowl filled with stew and a steaming cup of coffee sat on top. "Sit. You should have some lunch before you head out."

"Looks great, Gwen, thank you."

"My pleasure, dear."

Jacob finished scraping his bowl clean when Clint arrived. He stopped next to one of the picnic tables and motioned the group over.

"Francois, Davie, and Jacob, huddle up. We need to make contact with civilization, or we're going to get overrun here. First things first, I want to check the perimeter, then see about getting out to the highway. Jacob, did you find a map?"

"Yeah." Jacob pulled the backpack up from the ground beside him, withdrew the map, and held it up.

Clint took it from him and spread it out on the tabletop. He slid his finger over the tattered paper in arcing circles until he found their community. "Okay, we're here. What I was thinking is we head south, then loop around counter clockwise. We'll come back up on Eagle, and if the going isn't too bad, go up Sumner a'ways. I want to come around north of the Benson's place, then over to the highway. We'll see what we can from there. Worst case, we circle back to home base before sunset. That work for everybody?"

Francois shrugged. "Sure."

Jacob nodded.

Davie grabbed the brim of his hat and pushed it high on his head. "You know better than me, man."

"All right. Gwen and Harold, you're still okay to hold down the fort here?"

Gwen set a hand over a bulge in her jacket. "We'll be fine."

Clint smiled wide. "That's my girl."

"Do you need lunch before you head out?" Gwen gestured to the pot bubbling on the fire. "I warmed up some stew."

"No, I had something at the house. Thanks though."

When Clint walked past, the smell of his breath gave Jacob the impression it was of the liquid variety.

"Okay, let's go guys."

Rosana leaned into Francois. Pushing his fur-lined hood back, he cupped her face in his hands and pulled her in for a kiss. "I'll be home soon."

"Be safe. I love you."

"Je t'aime."

Jacob shouldered his backpack. Francois and Davie each had a pack of their own and one of the Benelli's. Clint adjusted the SKS over his shoulder, led the group past his house, and into the pristine snow.

At the edge of the tree cover, Davie called out. "*Wait*."

Jacob, Clint, and Francois halted in their tracks and looked back.

"I need to change."

Clint glared at his brother. "What? Why?"

"I'm wearing a red shirt." Davie held open his plaid jacket and lowered his voice. "Everyone knows the red shirts don't come back."

Francois looked to Jacob. "Is he kidding?"

Jacob frowned. "I don't think so."

Clint turned to leave. "Come on, we need to go."

"Clint? Guys?"

The three kept walking.

"*Jesus*. Fine, I'm coming." Davie bounced along the fresh tracks in the snow. "Wait up, will ya?"

————

Jacob looked back to the community as they cleared the tree line to the north. The wind had calmed. Smoke from the chimneys and central fire swirled and drifted high before fading away.

Davie called ahead. "Anything yet?"

Clint spit into the snow. "More tracks, and a fair bit of blood."

Jacob looped both thumbs under the straps of his pack and bent forward. "Hey, Harold told me the count from last night, but not much else. Did you guys see anything? I mean, the ash and all."

Clint snuck a quick glance behind him. "I don't know. We heard a couple explosions. More gunfire, probably from town. You know, the usual."

"The usual?"

"It is what it is, man. I still get the feeling we've got it easy out here." Clint motioned across the river. "I don't even want to know what's going on over there."

"Maybe you're right."

Jacob kept pace with Clint, focusing on each step. He scanned the area to the right. "I've been thinking. Something about this seems, not sure how to put it…organized."

"You think they're all working together?"

"No, not like that. I can't think of a better word. It's almost like a migration."

Francois shifted the shotgun to his opposite arm. "It's weird, yes? Except for the odd detour, they're mostly heading west."

Clint stopped and held up a hand. "Wait here." He trained his rifle on a body in the middle of the track ahead. He inched three steps forward and paused.

"Be careful, friend."

"Yeah, I don't think there's anything to worry about." Clint looked back over his shoulder. "Maybe cover me, just in case."

Francois waded sideways into the fresh snow and raised his shotgun. Clint eased up to the body. He nudged the leg, then stepped back and waited.

"It's okay, I don't think they're getting up."

Francois, Jacob, and Davie circled around the body. It looked to be mostly intact, but Jacob could not tell what damage existed before or what scavengers might have caused.

Francois scratched at his neck. "What do you think happened?"

Davie scanned behind him from the corner of his eye. "Think they bled out?"

Clint dropped to one knee, craning his neck to look around the body and feel the pockets. "Could be." He found a cell phone in the front pants pocket and handed it to Jacob. Jacob searched in and around the case. Tucked in the back, he found a folded twenty and a license. "Stephanie Cole. Rochester."

"Phone got a charge?"

Jacob pressed all the buttons. The outline of a battery, with a thin red line on the left side, flashed across the screen before it went dark. "Nope." He dropped the phone onto the body and put the license in his front pocket. Reaching behind, he wiggled the map from a side pocket of the pack, made a mark with one of the pencils, then tucked it back inside.

Davie coughed into his arm and faced away. "Damn, I thought that was a dude."

Francois frowned. "I didn't want to guess."

Clint ran a thumb under the rifle strap on his shoulder. "Let's keep moving."

———

The convoy continued to the main road, then turned east. Three hundred meters out, the snow deepened to the point of being impassable. They saw no signs that anyone had been through, so they turned back. At the road adjacent to the Benson's property, the group headed north. A few minutes in, Francois spotted a clearing beside the road and suggested they stop for a rest. Two fallen trees crossed over each other. Francois sat down on a low spot and leaned the shotgun beside him. Stretching out one leg, he unzipped his jacket. "Man, getting a little warm."

Jacob and Davie each found a spot to sit. Jacob pulled his toque off and set it on his knee. "It's better than freezing to death, I guess."

Francois removed a thermos from his pack. "I'm just never happy. That's what Rosana says anyway." He popped the cup off and unscrewed the cap. He poured the cup half full and took a sip. "Ah, c'est bon."

"Good coffee?"

"Coffee is shit. The bourbon's not bad." Francois smiled and winked at Jacob.

Clint dug into his jacket and pulled a package of cigarettes out from his breast pocket. Putting his arm up, he rested against the end of one of the downed trees. "Hey, Frenchie, you got the time?"

Francois set his cup down and pulled the sleeve back on his right arm. "One-fifty."

"Shit, already?"

Francois shrugged and tucked his sleeve back into his glove.

Davie leaned forward on his elbows. "Are we still sticking to the plan?"

"Yeah." Clint eyed the road. "The tracks lead up that way. We need to keep going."

Jacob took a generous bite from one of his sandwiches. Still chewing, he drained a half bottle of water. "It's been kind of quiet, don't you think?"

Unlit cigarette dangling at the corner of his mouth, Clint stripped the bark off a nearby branch. "Naw, I think this is normal. How many have you seen during the day?"

Francois shrugged. "None so far."

"Exactly."

Eyes darting between Clint and Francois, Davie chimed in, "Well, there was the one…"

"But we had to find him, right? He wasn't out wandering."

"Yeah, I guess."

"That's something about them, I figure. It's why I want to be back before sundown, and why I wasn't worried about leaving the geriatric crew to keep watch."

"Little harsh, no?"

The beginning of a grin came to Jacob's lips. "Probably just upset that Harold showed them up."

Davie's expression soured.

Clint kept picking at his branch. "Whatever. How about you take watch tonight? See how you handle it."

Jacob shrugged. "Sure."

Clint waved him off. "Listen, like I was saying earlier, I think we're lucky. If we keep our eyes open and our shit together, we just might get through this."

Thick gray clouds crawled in from the east, concealing the sun. Clint inspected the changing sky. "We should get going."

"You're the boss." Francois snapped the cup back on his thermos and shouldered the shotgun. "Let's go then."

THIRTY-ONE

Buildings and infrastructure faded to vast swaths of powder white fields and clutches of frosted trees. They cut a clear line against the flat gray sky. The unending snowfall hid the tracks of any attempt to escape along the north road. With special attention paid to the patterns in the surface, Alex managed to stay between the ditches.

He yawned and rubbed a knuckle at his eye. At the same time, uneven ground shook the wheel in his hand. He feathered the accelerator and spun the steering wheel to correct as the back end of the SUV lost its path. The engine labored, and the traction control icon flashed on the dash. He put his foot to the floor, but it could not stop the front tires from relenting to the snow. Alex braced. His mother jolted forward against the seatbelt as the small SUV came to a stop with one wheel edging away from the shoulder. He slammed his palm against the steering wheel.

"*Fuck.*"

Eileen's head lolled, a fleck of spittle at the corner of her mouth. Her shallow breath hitched, then she coughed, open mouthed. Alex watched as she twisted her body toward the side window and settled.

He clenched his teeth, focused back on the road, and wrenched the transmission into reverse. The SUV hitched sideways as the wheels spun. Letting off of the throttle, he clicked the shifter to drive. Again, the vehicle fought, but instead of moving toward the open road, inched closer to the ditch. The engine calmed, and it settled into the ruts left by the attempt.

Alex watched through the windshield, eyes hard and jaw tight. Through the falling snow, he noticed the first signs of the sky darkening to the east. He tilted his head back and held his hands over his face. Scenarios, and images of the few options remaining for a safe escape, scrolled through his mind.

Next to him, Eileen straightened in her seat. The leather creaked under her weight. Alex bent his head to face his mother. Her chest rose and fell in long, slow movements. Unsticking her eyelids, she looked sidelong at Alex with a spec of red building at the corner of her eye.

THIRTY-TWO

Entering a cluster of trees, the group spread out. Clint and Francois stayed on opposite sides, with Davie in the middle, and Jacob trailing behind. Soon, they were past the northern tip of the Benson's property. Clint did not feel the need to go back to their house. From what could be seen, it looked unchanged since they led Deborah out the day before.

Branches cast strange shadows as they swayed in the gentle breeze. Jacob scanned between the gaps in the trees, doing his best to ignore his aching legs and numb toes. Dense snow started to crust, and their crunching footsteps echoed around them.

Francois paused and raised his shotgun. "Whoa, what's that?"

Davie stopped, with his eyes wide. He fumbled his shotgun but managed to point the barrel straight. "Clint, over there."

The group zeroed in on a dark mass a few meters ahead of them, half hidden by the trunk of a tree. Clint pushed up on the brim of his hat. "Hold up."

Rifle across his back, Clint moved forward to a body face down in the snow. Its legs splayed out at odd angles, and arms were crossed underneath. Clint took a few steps around the body before nudging it with the tip of his boot. He looked further on ahead and to both sides, then waved the other three over.

"Jacob, check this one." He pointed into the trees. "There's another one over there. Looks like a few more up ahead, too. Let's be quick about it, we don't have a lot of time."

Jacob collected five new pieces of identification by the time they cleared the trees. They found six others without, but he marked them on his map just the same.

As they stood in the ditch and stared up at the highway, Davie lifted his hat and scratched his damp hair. "Well, we made it, I guess."

"Thank God." Francois fanned his open jacket, cooling sweat along his back. "I'm getting a little tired of playing in the snow."

"We're not done yet, Frenchie." Clint patted Francois on the back and climbed toward the road.

Francois shuffled the shotgun to his left hand and adjusted the weight of his pack. He followed along Clint's footprints and muttered under his breath. "Tabernak."

Davie smiled and fell in behind. Jacob looked back the way they had come. Shadows stretched, creeping among the trees. His heartrate increased as the potential for what could not be seen ran through his mind. He quickly spun and rushed to catch up with the others.

When he crested the rise onto the highway, he saw Clint and Davie surveying the area. Francois laid spread eagle on the ground a short distance from them. He held one hand above his eyes to shield them from the light and falling snow.

Jacob pursed his lips. "You okay?"

Francois' breath came shallow and fast. "I'm too old for this shit."

Jacob checked both ways along the road. "Yeah."

Snow blanketed the highway, but it did not rise past their knees as it had during portions of their journey. Tire tracks marred the northbound lane but faded as snow continued to fall.

Jacob walked up behind Clint and Davie. "Anything interesting?"

Clint gestured along the road. "There's a vehicle stuck up that way. Hard to tell how long it's been there. To be honest, I'm surprised they made it as far as they did. Don't see anyone around at the moment." He motioned toward the ditch. "A few more bodies over there. Could just be trees or garbage, I guess." Turning, he nodded to the field in front of them. "See that barn?"

"Yeah."

"We saw something moving around the back."

"Like what?"

"Not sure. Didn't get a good look."

"Are you sure it wasn't a bird or something?"

"Yeah, I'm sure."

Jacob exhaled. He shifted his weight to the opposite leg and extended an ankle to stretch it. The barn was the only structure along the edge of the field. A small grove of trees stood to the south. To the northwest, a golf course hid beneath the snow cover, but it was obscured to the point he could not place its exact location. It would all make a beautiful picture, he thought, if you chose to ignore everything going on in the background.

"Hey, look." Davie pointed toward the barn. They watched a dark shadow slip in through a crack in the big sliding door.

Clint and Jacob looked to each other. Clint motioned toward the barn. "You in?"

Jacob turned his face to the sky and closed one eye against the falling snow. "It's going to be dark soon, we need to hurry."

"We don't have to go."

"I don't know, I think we do. What if it's someone that needs help?"

"All right then." Clint raised his head to look past Jacob. "Let's go, Frenchie. We're movin' on."

Francois sat up but leaned back on his palms. "No, I'm good."

"What d'ya mean?"

"I'll keep watch. You go."

"Serious?"

"Very."

Clint shrugged. "Okay, let's go, you two."

Clint and Davie flanked Jacob as they approached the barn. Fresh tracks in the snow led up to the door.

Clint squeezed the brim of his hat. "Davie, you go around the right side. I'll keep an eye on the left side, just to be safe."

With a nod, Davie raised his shotgun and moved around the front right corner of the barn. He continued down the length, staying close to the red painted boards. At the farthest corner, he leaned tight to the wall. After taking a breath, he jumped out with the barrel of his gun swinging in all directions. The area appeared to be free of any would-be attackers, so he walked behind the barn and out of view.

Jacob kept his voice low. "I think he's watched too many bad cop shows."

Clint grinned. "Everyone has their thing, I guess."

Clint and Jacob looked along the left side of the barn. Falling snow hovered and swirled, but they saw no sign of Davie. With every breath, Jacob's heart thumped faster in his chest. "It's been too long, right?"

Clint slid the rifle free of his shoulder. "Yeah." He took two steps forward. "Davie? Where you at?"

They waited, but heard no response.

"Shit."

Staying close to the barn, Clint walked up to an old abandoned pickup truck halfway down. Tell-tale red stains tainted the tracks around it. As he neared the rear corner, a figure leaped out at him.

"*Ha.*"

Clint staggered back. "*Jesus Christ, Davie.*"

Jacob put out an arm and leaned against the barn with his head down. "Holy shit."

Clint grabbed Davie by his collar and pulled him around to the front corner. "Nearly gave me a fuckin' heart attack, ya dink."

"Jeez, lighten up already."

"Lighten up? Have you forgotten what we're doing out here?"

Davie frowned. "Sorry, just trying to have a little fun. There ain't nothin' out that way, just open field."

"Wait," Jacob raised a hand to the brothers, "did you hear that?"

They stood silent, listening. From inside, they heard the

soft creaking of pressure on wood boards. Clint kept his voice hushed and leaned toward Jacob. "Think it's just settling or something?"

"You saw. Someone's in there."

"Think it's one of those things?"

Jacob looked to the weathered concrete pad in front of the door. "There's no blood, if that means anything."

"What do we do?"

"I don't know. We go in, I guess."

Clint sighed. "Okay, you get the door. I'll be ready."

Closing in on the large wooden door, Jacob raised his hand to the pressed metal handle. Clint turned to Davie, motioned him away, then stepped to the opposite side. Clint firmed his stance and lifted his rifle. Wind picked up from the east, and the world around them washed with flowing white. Clint focused his attention on the barn and nodded. Jacob tightened his grip on the handle and pulled. Clint stepped forward, but froze when Davie screamed out behind him. After a moment of hesitation, Jacob threw his full weight into the door and slammed it shut.

Clint and Jacob turned to see Davie on the ground, pinned by a squirming, bloody figure. Davie jammed his forearm against the man's throat. His free hand searched for the shotgun sinking in the snow beside him. The man growled as he bit at the air in front of Davie's face. Clint rushed to kick the attacker in the ribs as hard as he could. The man landed on his back next to Davie. Clint shoved the barrel of the SKS against the man's forehead and pulled the trigger.

Davie scrambled to all fours, heaving and spitting blood onto the snow. Clint dropped down beside his brother. "Davie, are you okay?"

Davie looked up to Clint, his face dappled with crimson.

"Fucker bled all over me." He spit again. "Don't think he got me, though."

Jacob hurried to join them. "Guys, *incoming.*"

Two figures emerged from the grove of trees and came at them on either side. Movement through the dense snowfall showed two more following. Clint raised his SKS and fired. The two in the lead fell before the click of the hammer signaled it had run out of ammo. "*Goddamn it.*" Clint slipped the pack off his back and pulled out a small cardboard box. Taking a knee, he added rounds to the magazine.

Jacob rushed to pull the Benelli from the snow next to Davie. He tucked the shotgun into his shoulder and squeezed the trigger. Nothing happened.

Clint shouted. "*The safety.*"

Jacob looked along the shotgun and flipped the tab near the trigger guard. He lifted it and sighted on a woman closing fast. He squeezed the trigger. It kicked more than he expected, and he almost lost his footing. The woman jerked back and stopped two meters away. Scattershot had blemished her face and took her ear. Shredded flesh showed the muscle and bone on her left shoulder. Blood spewed from her mouth and down her chin. She snarled and lunged for him. A loud crack shook the air, and the crown of her skull split. Her eyes rolled back, and her jaw fell loose as she collapsed. Jacob saw Francois waving from the edge of the highway. Clint slammed the loaded magazine of the SKS shut and fired on the fourth. The man spun sideways from the impact and fell flat on his back. Two shots came in succession from the road. At the edge of the trees, another silhouette fell to the ground.

Clint took deep gulping breaths as he sighted the rifle on the trees. "Everyone okay?"

Davie stood on shaky knees. "Yeah."

"Think so." Jacob glanced to the woman prone on the ground. "Jesus, she was a cop."

"Yeah, well, nobody is safe, I guess." Clint turned and waved to Francois. He got a thumbs-up in return. "We need to get the hell out of here. Let's check the barn, then book it home."

Davie's voice wavered. "Clint, man, I think we should just go."

"Shut up, Davie. Jacob, let's do this."

Jacob moved to the door of the barn. Clint nodded and pulled the door open. Jacob crept inside with the shotgun raised. It smelled of old straw and mouse droppings. He shifted to the side and put his back against the inside of the door. Clint passed across the threshold and scanned the darkness.

Jacob swallowed hard. "Hello? It's okay, you can come out. We have a safe place, but we need to leave now."

Clint inched forward, the aim of his rifle constantly searching. He spotted movement in the shadows as a low growl came from one of the closed stalls. A quiet voice echoed from the back of the barn.

"Jacob?"

THIRTY-THREE

Through the crosshairs of a scope, the group moved across the road and down into the ditch. With the muted glow of the setting sun at their backs, they continued along the way they had come.

Alex lowered the scope and let it hang from the strap around his neck. He adjusted the respirator built into his balaclava and the seal of his goggles. After two deep breaths to confirm his vision stayed clear, he cinched the cuffs of his gloves. The matte black handle of a pistol stuck out from a holster at his leg. He raised one hand to rest on the edge of the SUV's hatch and paused.

Eileen slumped forward in the passenger seat. Flecks of blood and dark gore spotted the windshield and the side window. Alex removed a balled up t-shirt and bottle of lighter fluid from the back of the SUV, then slammed the hatch shut.

The windows on the driver's side were halfway down. He stopped at the rear door and tossed the t-shirt onto the back seat. Next, he pulled the cap from the lighter fluid and sprayed a stream over the shirt and seat. When the bottle ran dry, he dropped it in as well. Alex flipped open a pocket on his vest and pulled out a pack of matches. He struck the end of one, watched it burn for a moment, then flicked it into the backseat. On his way past, he picked up his bag from the ground behind the SUV and walked down the road.

The sound of snow compacting under heavy boots echoed in the silence as the fire gained strength. Alex kept a steady pace along the ruts as heavy flakes danced around him. He stopped where the group crossed and held the strap of his bag over his chest. He looked to the barn and the mess of bodies in front of it, then focused across the highway, and followed the tracks in the snow leading to the east.

THIRTY-FOUR

Jacob stifled a yawn as he headed to the fire.

Clint adjusted the burning logs with a bent stick. He looked up and tossed it into the fire. "You gonna be all right, there?"

Jacob rubbed at his neck. "I think so."

Clint motioned to Jacob's house. "Everyone settled in?"

"Yeah."

"Good." Clint, still with the SKS resting over his shoulder, walked to the nearest picnic table. He grabbed one of the camouflage shotguns by the forestock. "I sent Harold home. We should get some practice in before it gets too busy."

"Sure."

Clint held the gun out. "I set up a bit of a blind up the road."

Jacob reached out for the shotgun and fumbled the strap over his shoulder.

"You sure you don't want a coffee or somethin'?"

Jacob shook his head and looked along the road. "Let's go."

They walked into the darkness along the same paths that brought trouble to the community each night. As his eyes adjusted, Jacob focused on the ground in front of his feet and counted the blood spots. Halfway toward the main road, two pallets stood at a right angle to each other in the snow. Space enough for two people to stand had been cleared. Out in the relatively untouched snow, an old ball cap hung from a thick tree branch.

"Rule number one. If you've got a gun in your hand, treat it like it's loaded. All that really means is, don't point it at anyone you're fond of."

Jacob slipped the shotgun forward and took it in both hands. He held it with the barrel pointing to the ground.

"Aww, thanks, man." Clint cracked a wry smile. "Now, try aiming for the hat."

Jacob looked to the branch. He stepped forward with his left foot, set the butt in the hollow of his shoulder, and lowered his head to aim.

"Rule number two. You ain't no fuckin' summer blockbuster action hero." Clint kicked at Jacob's trailing foot. "Square up a little."

Jacob corrected his footing, so his body faced the target straight on.

"Go on." Clint waved a hand. "Give it a go."

Jacob repositioned.

"Elbow down. Bring the buttstock up a little." Clint took a step back. "Good. Okay, rock and roll."

Jacob shifted in place and lowered his cheek against the stock. His finger rested against the trigger.

"Stop holding your breath."

Jacob slowly released air through his mouth and looked to Clint from the corner of his eye. Clearing his throat, he settled in. The shotgun popped, and his shoulder jerked back. The hat on the branch remained untouched.

"Squeeze don't pull. Straight back."

Jacob returned his concentration to the hat. After a short pause, the barrel erupted once more. The branch holding the hat, and the edge of the brim, shredded and fell away.

Clint slapped a hand against Jacob's back. "Nice shot."

Off in the formless dark, a voice screamed out in rage. The breeze carried sounds of movement through the snow. Jacob turned to see Clint striding away with the SKS in the crook of his arm.

"Let's move. You'll get plenty more practice soon enough."

THIRTY-FIVE

Jacob reclined in his chair with both hands wrapped around a fresh mug of coffee. He watched the low flames of the fire flicker in and out with the wind. The rising sun broke the horizon, fighting through haze and low clouds.

Harold approached the circle and stood beside him. "How're you holding up?"

Jacob's bruised shoulder twitched to a half shrug. "Okay. Been running on adrenaline for too long. Starting to wear off."

"You all made it. That's something."

"We got lucky on the way back. Only crossed paths with a few, but we managed to lay low until they moved on. Heard others but stayed out of their way."

Harold nodded. "What's the count here?"

"I don't know. Too many. Mostly from Fort Erie, but a couple from Port Colborne. One of them Clint recognized, said he knew his sister. She works at the liquor store on Thompson. I think his name was Everett. That's all he said though."

Harold studied Jacob and chewed on the air for a moment. "Why don't you head in, I'll keep an eye out here."

"You sure?"

"It'll be fine." Harold smiled. "Tell Gwen it's time for breakfast while you're at it."

"Okay, I will."

Before going into the house, Jacob checked on the generator and filled the tank. Inside the front door, he pulled the toque from his head and kicked off his snow-crusted boots. At the kitchen table, Gwen worked on a game of solitaire.

"Morning."

"Good morning, dear."

"How's she doing?"

"Fine, as far as I can tell. She ate a little before going to sleep. Drank all your water, too."

"Oh, well, that's all right."

Gwen paused with a frown on her face, then swept her hand across the table, collecting the cards. She sorted them into a pile and snapped them down on their edge. "Okay, I'll start some breakfast and boil more water. Be back shortly."

"Sounds good. Thanks, Gwen."

Jacob unzipped his jacket and sat on the recliner in the living room. He sank back and rubbed at his eyes.

A mound of blankets on the couch showed signs of life. An arm emerged and hung down to touch the floor, then Mati raised her head from the pillow and let out a sharp exhale. She kept her eyes thin against the dim light seeping in through the windows. Sitting up, she ran her fingers through her hair and shook it loose. "Hey."

"Morning. Want some coffee?"

"Sure."

Jacob stifled a groan as he peeled himself from the plush cushions. In the kitchen, he took the lid off a small saucepan, poured the contents into an empty mug, and brought it to the living room.

"Sorry, probably a little cold. It's been sugared though."

"That's okay. Thanks."

Sam curled up at the end of the couch with a paw over her nose. One eye followed Jacob as he moved past and handed the mug to Mati.

"I'll go get some hot water so you can clean up. Breakfast should be ready soon. Anything else I can grab for you?"

"No, I should be fine."

"Okay."

Jacob zipped his coat, slipped his boots on, and went to join the group outside. Deborah, Penny, and Harold sat huddled around the crackling fire. Gwen puttered about, sorting pots and arranging utensils.

Penny turned in her chair. "Good morning. How's your lady friend doing?"

"Okay, all things considered."

Gwen shuffled past, watching Penny over her glasses. "Water is over there, dear. I'll dish up a plate for her when you get back."

"Thanks, Gwen." Jacob grabbed a towel and wrapped it around the handle of the simmering pot sitting to the side of the coals.

He walked the steaming pot inside and left it next to the kitchen sink. Mati sat up with the blanket over her shoulders. Sam laid in front of her, keeping an eye on the activity in the room.

"There's a couple towels on the counter. I pulled out a sweater, and some other clothes I thought might fit, if you need to change. You can come out when you're done, or I can bring a plate in, it's up to you."

"I'll come out. Thanks."

At the circle, Jacob heaped a paper plate tall with sausages and diced potatoes doused in ketchup.

"Don't forget the fruit." Gwen pointed to two open cans of fruit cocktail on the picnic table. "Just be sure to save some for the girl."

"I will." Jacob took a seat and ate.

He watched his empty plate burn in the fire as Mati and Sam came out of the house. Mati walked slow and kept her head down. She sat in the empty chair beside Jacob and stretched her hands out to warm them. Sam took a hesitant sniff around, then perched beside her.

"Good morning, dear." Gwen held a loaded plate out for Mati. "How are you doing?"

"Okay." Mati set the plate on her lap. She picked up a sausage and held it down for Sam.

"Your stomach all right?"

"Better." Mati took the fork and stabbed at the potatoes.

"Do you want to talk about what happened?"

Mati looked around the group as she chewed.

Jacob cleared his throat. "Maybe we should give her some time to eat."

"No. It's okay." Mouth half-full, Mati loaded in another forkful of potatoes. She skewered a sausage on to her fork and set the plate down in front of Sam.

Jacob stood to pour a fresh cup of coffee. He swirled the dark liquid in the mug and waited.

Mati scratched the top of Sam's head. "We got as far as Kingston." Mati looked to Jacob, then off into the distance. "I caught a ride that I shouldn't have and ended up in Dundas."

Jacob shifted the mug to his opposite hand. "Is that when the power went out?"

Mati nodded. "I stayed with them the first night, but I started hearing things. People said it was some sort of attack and that roads were being closed. I got scared, and I left." She fought a quiver in her chin. "I didn't know where else to go. It was a stupid move, but I…" Mati wiped her nose with the sleeve of her sweater. "I couldn't find a ride after St. Catherine, so I decided to walk. We did okay for a while, then those sick people started showing up. We learned how to stay out of their way."

Jacob gave a thin-lipped smile. "I'm glad we found you."

"Me too."

"Well," Gwen set her hands on her knees and leaned forward, "if we keep this up, we're going to run out of beds. First Deb, and now you. The more the merrier, I guess."

Mati fidgeted in her seat and pulled her hands into her sleeves. She stared at the ground in front of her. "Listen, I'm sort of running low on…supplies."

Jacob squinted. It took a moment to make the connection. "Oh." He glanced to Gwen and Penny with wide eyes.

Gwen laughed. "Don't look at us, dear."

Penny covered her mouth with one hand and turned away, snickering.

Jacob frowned. "I, uh…"

Gwen pushed herself up and out of her chair. "Come on, I think Erica will be able to help you out."

Mati stood but kept her eyes low. "Thanks."

Gwen put a hand against Mati's back and led her to Clint and Erica's front door. Sam followed close behind.

Jacob helped clean up breakfast and positioned large pots

of water at the fire. He dried his hands on a spare towel. "Penny, are we good here?"

"I think so. Go on, get some rest."

Jacob draped the towel from one end of the picnic table. "Yeah, maybe." He looked south to the end of the circle. "I think I'll go check on Mati first. Maybe see how Davie is doing, too."

Jacob retrieved his gloves from his chair and stuffed them in his jacket pocket. His feet dragged as he walked up the path to Clint and Erica's house. The indent left by Clint's truck in the driveway had filled in. Someone carved a happy face into the packed snow on the Camaro windshield, but later changed it to a frown. Sam waited on the front porch. Her ears perked when Jacob neared.

"Hello, Miss Samantha. She'll be out soon, don't worry."

Sam stretched her neck and sniffed at Jacob as he knocked on the door three times. The faded curtain covering the small window pulled to one side, then the door opened. Erica smiled and waved Jacob in as she rubbed at a dry stain on her sweatpants. Even among the chaos, her presence was warm. Jacob kicked the instep of his boots against each other to knock the snow off.

"Don't worry about your boots."

"You sure?"

"Oh, yeah. The place is a mess already."

Mati and Gwen sat at the kitchen table. Jacob raised a hand in greeting. Gwen waved back. Mati gave a shy smile.

Jacob slid his hands in his pockets and turned to Erica. "How are you holding up?"

Erica reached up to adjust the loose knot of wavy hair behind one ear. "Making the best of it. The kids are going a little stir crazy, though. Hayden's down for his nap. Allena and Parker are building a fort in our bedroom closet." Erica rolled her eyes. "Clint says those people don't come out during the day, so I'm going to see if we can get them out for some fresh air at lunch. Still a little nervous."

"I understand. It's a scary situation."

"Yeah." Erica crossed her arms and looked at the floor. "Anyway, Clint just got in from checking on Davie, and he's washing up. He'll be out soon."

"Sounds good. Thanks."

Picking up toys as she went, Erica gave a strained smile and disappeared into the kitchen. Jacob moved to the living room and settled on one end of the leather sofa. The green cushions sagged, and the color had worn away at spots on the arm. A matching chair beside it looked to be in even worse shape. Marker scribbles and paint splatter decorated a small, molded plastic table and two chairs in the corner. The abstract creations tacked to the wall above must have caused them. Tall floor speakers flanked a massive flat screen TV mounted on the inside wall. A cabinet under the TV held stereo equipment and an assortment of video game systems. All the expense and importance given to them meant little as they sat lifeless and unusable.

A young boy trotted into the room with a wide smile on his face. Juice stained his lips. His eyes sparkled full of joy as he stopped in front of Jacob. "Hi."

"Hey, bud."

Allena screeched from down the hall. "Hurry, Parker, *they're coming.*"

Parker giggled, turned, and ran back the way he came. Clint mussed his hair as he passed.

"Morning." Clint walked in and dropped down onto the battered leather chair.

Jacob lifted a tired hand to greet him. "Hey, how's it going?"

"Better than you by the looks of it. Didn't you get any sleep?"

"Not yet. I wanted to talk to Mati before I turned in."

Clint looked toward the kitchen, then back to Jacob. "So, what's goin' on with that, anyway?"

Jacob gave a half-hearted shrug. "Nothing's going on. She was thumbing it, so I gave her a ride. We spent a couple days together. That's about it."

Clint raised an eyebrow and smiled. "Oh, yeah?"

Jacob scowled. "It's not like that. Jesus, what's wrong with you people?"

Clint melted back in the chair. "No harm meant. It must have been something for her to come all that way in the middle of this mess, right?"

"Maybe. I don't know. I think we're just damaged in similar ways."

"Like kindred spirits or some shit?"

Jacob shrugged. "Yeah. Speaking of damaged, how's Davie doing?"

"I don't know, man. I was just out checking on him, said he wasn't feeling well. Looks almost as bad as you."

Jacob grinned. "Wow, thanks. Do you think yesterday was a little much for him, or is it something else?"

"I don't know." Clint focused out the living room window. "Anyway, he said he'd be out in a bit."

Jacob yawned into the back of his hand, then leaned forward with his elbows on his knees. "Damn."

"You should really get some rest, man."

"I really should." Jacob put his hands down on the cushion and pushed himself upright. "See you tonight?"

"Sure."

Jacob lumbered to the kitchen. He put a hand on the back of Gwen's chair and waited for a pause in the conversation. "Hey, I'm going to close my eyes for a bit."

Mati pushed her chair back from the table. "I'll come too."

"You can stay, it's okay."

"No, I should check on Sam."

"Okay." Jacob waved to Gwen and Erica. "Have a good afternoon, ladies."

"You too, hope you get some rest. It was very nice to meet you, Mati."

Mati smiled. "You too. Thanks again for…you know." Her cheeks flushed with color.

"Any time, sweetie. See you in a bit."

Sam fell in behind Mati and Jacob as they walked down the porch steps and over to the fire. Francois smiled and waved when they approached. "Good morning."

"Hey, Francois."

"And how are you doing today, young lady?"

Mati drew her hands up into her sleeves. "Good."

Francois nodded. "Good."

Jacob held his hands to the fire. "Where did everyone else get off to?"

"Well, Penny and Deb took Harold off to warm up. If they were a few decades younger, I'd make a joke, but…" Francois made a face like he was about to be ill.

Jacob stifled a laugh.

"Nick just went to take some wood in to the wife. Rosana is fixing her makeup." Francois' eyes went wide. "I wish I was kidding. The love of my life, she is, but sometimes I shake my head."

Davie stumbled out from behind Clint's house, shielding his eyes with a flat hand over his brow. Sweat stains soaked his once white t-shirt, and a wrinkled pair of jeans showed new tears along the legs. Loose shoelaces flopped around as he trudged toward the group.

Behind Mati, Sam stood with her ears laid back, and the ridge of hair along her spine raised. Jacob walked to intercept Davie at the fire's edge. "Hey, man, are you okay?"

"Yeah, think so. Why the hell is it so bright?"

Francois looked to the overcast sky above Davie's head. "Is it?"

"My eyes hurt. Where's Clint?"

Shifting his weight between his feet, Jacob crossed his arms. "At home."

Davie licked his dry lips. "Oh."

"Listen, maybe you should get back to your trailer. I'll go get Clint for you, okay?"

"Tired of the camper." Davie searched around out of the corner of his eye. "Can't sleep. Too hot."

"Crack a window or something. You shouldn't be out here dressed like that."

Davie cleared his throat. "Okay." He coughed into his hand, and a wet rattle sounded in his chest. Wiping his hand on his jeans, he wandered back the way he came.

Jacob and Francois exchanged worried looks. Jacob started to follow, but Davie stopped. His eyes held no emotion. "It's okay. I'm fine."

Jacob and Francois watched him walk around the far corner of the house and disappear.

"What the hell was that?"

Jacob exhaled. "Not sure."

Francois frowned. "I'll go get Clint. You head in."

"Yeah. Thanks." Jacob rubbed at his eye with a closed hand. "I'll be out before dinner, but come and get me if anything happens, okay?"

"You got it."

Jacob gave a weak smile and half-raised his hand to Mati. "See you in a bit."

Mati's lips went tight, and she nodded.

THIRTY-SIX

Alex lifted his goggles to the top of his head and raised the scope to his eye. The image appeared grainy and dim, but he could still make out details. A tangle of tree trunks and garbage blocked the road into the nearby community. Similar stacks littered the space between some of the houses as well. Thin streams of smoke rose from a central fire. He counted three residents out, but the number often changed.

Alex lowered the scope and sat up, resting his arms on his raised knees. Shrouded by dense clouds to the east, the sun fought its way higher in the sky. Soon, it would be safe to tuck away and get some rest. He scanned around the clutch of trees for signs of movement, then focused on the trees themselves. The hours spent building up snow walls and covering tracks proved worth the effort. It allowed him a sense of security not known in recent memory.

Twice, he considered approaching the community and leaving his hidden sanctuary. They welcomed the woman, after all, seemingly with open arms. He was not the woman, though. Years of disappointment taught him to only count on himself. It made him capable in ways the others were not.

Alex pulled on the top of his head to crack the joints in his neck. He stood and tucked the scope into his vest, then disappeared back among the trees.

THIRTY-SEVEN

Jacob walked out of his bedroom, wiping the sleep from his eyes. He found Mati cross-legged on the couch with a book open on her lap. She turned a page and rested her chin on a closed fist. On the floor, Sam laid with her head bent around to her tail, and all four legs stuck up in the air. Her tongue pushed against her teeth and poked out at the corner.

"Hey."

Mati looked up and tucked a strand of hair behind her ear. "Hey."

"Everything all right out here?"

"Sure."

Jacob stretched his arms to the ceiling and groaned. "Well, I'm going to head out. You wanna come?"

Mati's mouth twisted down on one side, and she shrugged.

"I'll check on you in a bit, then." Jacob turned to go.

"Wait..." Mati straightened and sighed. "Sit down." She looked up into Jacob's eyes. "Please."

Eyebrow raised, Jacob stepped in front of the recliner and sat. "What's up?"

Mati set her book aside and held her hands on her lap. "I just…" she frowned and looked out beyond the living room window, "I wanted to, you know…talk."

"Okay. About what?"

"You opened up to me, so maybe it's my turn, okay?"

Jacob watched through narrowed eyes and waited.

Mati sank back, clutched the ends of her sleeves in her fingers, and took a deep breath. "My mom was seventeen when she met my dad. She got pregnant pretty quick. I don't remember much, but Mom said things were good at first. Dad got us a place of our own. It was a good neighborhood. Safe. It was everything we needed. He was a mechanic. Mom did housework and laundry, that kind of thing.

"I was five or six when Dad started staying out late. Sometimes, he didn't come home at all. Mom started to drink, and they fought a lot after that. It's all I remember about that time. Eventually, Dad left. Over the years, Mom's drinking got worse. She had a lot of boyfriends. Some, I think for money. I didn't like being home, wherever that was at the time, but it was hard being out, too. I didn't fit in with people my own age, so I'd hang out with the older kids and get into trouble a lot. I ended up dropping out of school."

Mati took a deep breath before continuing. Her voice wavered. "I started making some really bad choices. On my sixteenth birthday, I let my guard down and got drunk. I slept with a guy I barely knew and got pregnant. I had no idea what to do, so I drank or took whatever I could find." Mati stared at the floor and wiped her eyes. "I lost the baby."

Jacob opened his mouth as if to speak, but closed it and adjusted himself in his seat, having no real idea what to offer in that moment.

"I've been doing better. Me and a couple of my girlfriends

got a place of our own. I graduated last year, and I started applying for scholarships, mostly in Montréal. Figured my dad would be a better influence." Mati wove her fingers together. "I guess you know how that turned out."

Jacob rested forward on his knees and nodded.

"By the time I realized how hard it was going to be to get here, to find you, it was too late. Trying to find someplace… safe, could have killed me. It's like I'm not allowed to know what it feels like."

Jacob shook his head. "I doubt that's true. You made it, didn't you?"

Mati sighed and pulled back on the sleeve of her sweater. "I don't know. Look what it's got us into."

Jacob paused. His eyes concentrated on Mati's forearm. "Are you okay?"

Mati looked to the parallel grooves, scabbed with blood, running from the inside of her wrist to the crook of her arm. She flushed and pulled her sleeve down. "It's nothing."

"Nothing?"

Mati focused hard on the book.

"What happened?"

"It's just a scratch."

Jacob pinched his lips tight.

Sensing his gaze, Mati raised her eyes. "I'm fine. I promise."

Jacob looked from her face to her arm, then got to his feet. "If that changes, you'll say something, right?"

Mati pursed her lips and nodded.

Jacob left the house.

Gwen steepled wood on the fire, wrapped her sweater tight against the chilled breeze, and sat on a lawn chair with a folded blanket on the seat. She smiled seeing Jacob walking to the fire. "Hello, dear. You're a bit early, aren't you?"

"Uh, yeah. A little. I woke up and couldn't get back to sleep." Jacob wrestled to close his jacket's zipper and snuck a glance to his front window. "Too much on my mind, I guess."

"Everything okay?"

"Hope so."

Gwen's eyes narrowed, but she nodded. "Well, there's a fresh pot of coffee by the fire, and we're just about done with getting dinner ready."

Rosana and Deborah fussed with the pots at the picnic table. Malena arrived at the circle in a puffy red jacket with a floral scarf wrapped over her head. She held a covered tray in her thick woven mitts.

Jacob smiled. "Hey, good to see you out."

Malena blushed. "Hello. Nice to be out, I suppose." She set the tray on the picnic table and helped Deborah move a full pot to warm on the fire.

"Gwen, is there anything I can do to help?"

"We've got it under control, dear."

"Okay. Has anyone checked on Davie lately?"

Gwen shook her head. "Not in a bit. He was out earlier, though."

Deborah clutched her hands in front of her. "Oh, that poor boy, he was in some sort of shape."

Rosana ran a hand over her hair and flipped it to one side. "Looked like he hadn't slept at all. Was acting a little crazy, too."

Gwen rested her arms on the camping chair. "You know, Erica had the kids out, and they were having a ball until Davie showed up. Scared Parker so bad, he ran off crying."

"Poor little guy."

"Anyway, Clint put an end to it pretty quick." Gwen motioned over her shoulder. "He sent his brother back off to his trailer."

Jacob raised an eyebrow. "Hopefully, he'll feel better after some rest."

"I hope so." The chair creaked as Gwen pushed herself up. "Okay, back to work. Jacob, can you go give Harold and Penny a fifteen-minute warning for dinner?"

"Yeah, sure."

"It's not much, but we're doing what we can."

"You know we all appreciate it."

Gwen gave a sad smile. "It's nice to have something to keep us occupied."

Jacob walked toward Harold's house, but he stopped short and looked over his shoulder. "You know what? I think I'm going to check on Davie first. Just in case."

"Fill your boots, dear."

Jacob nestled his hands deep in his jacket pockets and walked toward Clint and Erica's. As he passed the front bay window, Hayden slapped a wet fist against the glass, drawing designs in the squeaky smear. Jacob waggled his fingers and made a face. Hayden paused, then chirped and laughed loud as the drool flowed. A form in the shadow of the window startled Jacob. Erica smiled, cradling a large mug. Jacob's cheeks flared red, and he moved his hands back to his pockets. He offered a meek smile as he walked past the porch and around the corner of the house.

Nearing the trailer, Jacob's pace slowed. The small sliding windows were wide open, but the curtains remained closed. They fluttered in and out with the breeze. He paused in front of the door, put his left foot on the first step, and reached out to knock. A noise, like a handful of spoons forced down a garburator, shattered the silence. Jacob dropped his hand and released a stale breath. Davie snored in steady, rhythmic time. Jacob backed away from the trailer, turned, and ran around the front of the house.

––––––

At the circle, the breeze calmed. Smoke from the fire eased its erratic dance. Slow clouds drifted overhead, growing tall and blazing orange as the sun neared the horizon.

Mati yawned as she sank back in her chair and pulled the hood of her sweater over her eyes. Penny steadied her elbow on the arm of the chair and leaned her cheek against her open palm. Gwen interlaced her fingers over her stomach. Her chin tucked to her chest, and she rested her eyes. Jacob sat forward on his elbows and looked to the west.

"Think it might snow?"

Jacob turned to his right. Bundled up in his parka, Francois scratched at the side of his nose. Rosana stood close by his side. Her tailored black jacket ended at the waist of her tight-fitting jeans.

"Not sure. Maybe."

"Well, I guess we'll find out." Francois pointed a thumb over his shoulder. "I sent Clint home. He could use a night off."

"Sure, sounds good."

Francois walked to the wood pile and picked up a split log. He crouched down and set it on to the embers of the fire. Brushing his hands together, he sat in the empty chair beside Mati. "Well, young lady, what do you have to say for yourself?"

Mati looked sidelong at Jacob and shrugged. "Not sure."

"You've had quite the time of late, from what I hear."

"I guess."

"Forgive me for saying, but it sounds like you've had some disappointing times when it comes to family."

"You could say that."

"I'm sorry to hear. It's hard to understand, for me at least, how someone could make the choice to not be there for their own child."

Jacob sank back in his chair. "It is what it is. Unfortunately, we don't get to choose our family."

"This is true. I heard once that we get what we need, not what we want. I'm not so sure, but there might be something to it." Francois leaned in, extending his hands to the fire. "My father, his name was Andre, could have been one of those. He was very old-fashioned, didn't have much to do with us kids. He would leave for work early in the morning and come home late. After dinner, he would read his paper and listen to the radio, that was about it. Don't get me wrong, he took care of us in his own way. Food on the table, roof over our heads, that sort of thing. My mother, Liet, was a saint of a woman, raising three boys as well as she did. We put her through hell at times. You know, she wouldn't let us speak English in the house?"

Mati held a hand to her mouth and chewed on a fingernail. "Really?"

"She would bring out the belt, no joke. Wanted us to be proud of our heritage. You know how that goes."

Mati pulled her hands in her sleeves and rested on her elbows. "I think it's a good thing to be proud of. Not everyone gets that kind of foundation."

Francois' eyes softened. "I believe that you may be right. Thank you for your perspective."

A brief silence fell over the group. Gwen stood and

stretched her arms. She walked to the fire and checked on a simmering pot of water on the coals.

Jacob cleared his throat and straightened in his chair. "My parents were always on the move. When I was young, I wasn't really sure what they did. Consulting mostly. Building other people's businesses. Nothing you could hold in your hands." He looked down to the snow near his feet. "Dad died of a heart attack two days before his fifty-first birthday. The dirt had barely settled on his grave when Mom left to work as a missionary in South America. I was nineteen and basically left on my own. Everyone has a story, I guess."

Gwen gave a sad smile and moved to stand next to Penny. "That is true. I just hope you realize yours isn't over yet, and that things like family and home can mean a lot of different things."

Jacob looked around the circle. "I do." He wiped at one eye. "What about you guys? I don't remember if I've ever heard about your family. Are your parents still around?"

Gwen's eyebrows pinched together. She looked at Penny, then to Jacob. "My parents both passed in the early two-thousands."

Penny sat up in her chair. "My father died when I was a teenager. My mother is in an assisted living facility in Hamilton. She has dementia."

Jacob's eyes went wide. "But I thought…"

Gwen smiled, set a hand on Penny's shoulder, and gave a gentle squeeze. Penny lifted a hand and put it over Gwen's.

Jacob slouched forward. "You're not sisters."

"No. Sorry, dear."

Jacob gave an embarrassed smile and shook his head. "Don't be sorry, I'm the one that should be apologizing. It's just when Penny moved in, I was told…"

"Maybe your grandparents knew, maybe they didn't. People fill in the gaps with what makes sense to them. Either way, you were young, and it was a different time."

Jacob looked to Mati. She smiled a wide, toothy grin. "What?"

Mati shrugged. "I don't know. I'm not saying I was positive, but I picked up on it right away."

"Yeah, well, I never claimed to be the observant one in the group."

"That's a fact. I mean, you even stayed in their house and didn't notice."

Jacob smiled and covered his face with his hands amidst a round of light-hearted laughter and teasing remarks.

The group soon settled into quiet contemplation, but it lasted a short moment before Francois let out a loud exhale. "Well, the show's going to start soon, yes?"

Jacob looked to the setting sun but said nothing.

"Okay, then." Francois set a hand on Rosana's knee.

Rosana put her hand over Francois', then got to her feet. "Walk me home?"

"Of course."

She nodded to Mati, then glanced to the others. "Good night, everyone."

Francois followed Rosana along the path to their house. As they walked, she pulled a package of cigarettes from her jacket. She drew one out and balanced it on her lips, then continued up the steps to their porch and leaned against the frosted rail.

Francois stopped at the landing and looked into Rosana's eyes. "Mon amour."

Rosana lit the cigarette with a trembling hand, took a drag, and blew the smoke down. Her face was sober as she focused toward the fire.

Francois' gaze softened. "Oh, come now, don't be upset."

"It's dangerous, Francois. You know how I feel about all this."

"What are we supposed to do? Hide every night? Hope it will all pass us by? I need to do my part."

Rosana turned her dark eyes on Francois. "You need to be here with me."

"I will be with you soon. I promise."

Rosana looked back to the fire. She tossed the remains of her cigarette into the snow and went inside. The door slammed shut behind her.

"Je t'aime aussi." Francois ran his fingers through his hair and sighed.

Returning to the fire, he saw Penny walk up the steps to Harold's house. Jacob and Mati sat back from the flames. Sam curled up on a thin blanket at Mati's feet. Gwen stood to one side, her hands in her pockets. Francois took a shotgun from the picnic table and slid the strap over his shoulder. He shook away the chill on the air and held his hands over the fire. "What a day."

Gwen nodded. "It's been an interesting one, that's for sure."

"What is it anyway, Friday? Saturday?"

Mati shifted in her seat. "It's Thursday."

"Serious?" Francois sighed. "It feels like it's been a month already."

Twilight settled in. The group watched the smoke rise in silence. A gust of wind brought snowflakes and ash down around them in erratic patterns.

"Well, I think that's my cue." Gwen patted Jacob on his shoulder. "Good luck, boys."

"Have a good night, Gwen."

"I should go in too." Mati stood and crossed her arms tight against her body. "Come on, Sam."

Francois shifted the shotgun on his shoulder. "Good night."

Jacob raised a hand. "See you in the morning."

Mati gave an awkward smile. "Be safe." She turned and walked toward Jacob's house. Sam groaned and stretched before she followed Mati out of the circle.

Francois grinned at Jacob with one eyebrow raised.

"What?"

Francois turned away. "Nothing, nothing."

Jacob frowned. "I'm not sure why I have to keep repeating myself. It's not like that."

"If you say so, friend, but I've seen that look before."

"Come on. There was no look."

Francois shrugged and laughed to himself.

Jacob rose from his seat and went to the picnic table. He picked up both ammo boxes and flipped the lids back. "Not a lot left here."

"I forgot to check with Clint if he has more."

"Guess we need to be careful. Hopefully, it's a quiet night."

Francois lifted a chair and walked around the fire. He stuck it in the snow and sat facing the road into the community. "I guess we'll find out soon enough."

———

Jacob pulled up on his sleeve and raised his hand to catch the light from the fire. He sighed and lowered his arm. Time seemed to pass as slow as the snow fell.

Watching his breath drift away, Jacob caught movement in his peripheral. A blurred form shot out between the Miller's and the abandoned house. Francois saw it too and snapped the shotgun to his shoulder. An overweight Tabby sprinted across the circle, pushed through an opening in the snow, and hid under Jacob's truck.

Jacob's shoulders sagged. "Holy shit."

Francois lowered his gun. "Little bastard. I think Gwen owes me a pair of underwear."

Jacob turned at the sound of footsteps. Shadows morphed, and silhouettes became figures rushing toward the fire. Jacob sighted his shotgun. "Damnit, they're coming in on the path behind George and Darina's."

"Yeah, that's not the only place." Francois pointed in multiple directions up the road. He raised his gun and set his finger ready on the trigger. Jacob concentrated on the group coming in from the east. He saw three in all. The one in the rear scraped along the siding of the Miller's house.

"Stop right there. *Please.*"

The ragged breath, blood, and crowns of rising steam confirmed that no hope of a peaceful ending existed. One swung a broken arm as they advanced. Another had a crushed nose and oozing mouth with no teeth. Jacob pulled the trigger. The shot rang off in the dark. The group moving along the tire ruts stalled at the barricade of felled trees. Francois took aim and opened fire, three shots in a row. As the deafening noise echoed away, he knelt and plugged more rounds into the chamber. Jacob took a deep breath and planted his feet like Clint showed him. He fired again. Chunks of skull and brain matter sprayed over the Miller's front window, and the figure in the lead dropped to the ground. Even in the middle of a firefight, an irrational fear of what George would say about the mess flashed through Jacob's mind.

Francois stood, sited, and squeezed the trigger. Jacob took his third shot. The woman appeared younger than Jacob. Her head fell to her shoulder as part of her neck and jaw disintegrated. The third stumbled over the woman's body and fell to his hands and knees. He crawled forward, blood dripping down his chin. Jacob fumbled shells as he reloaded the Benelli, and they fell into the snow. He shoved his hand into his pocket, searching for more. A door slammed, and a thunderclap exploded behind him. The man crawling toward Jacob slumped to the ground. His arm twitched once before he stopped moving for good.

Jacob swiveled to see Harold braced against the railing of his front porch in little more than a bathrobe. His legs stuck up out of his rubber boots like toothpicks. "You boys fall back. Draw them in."

Jacob and Francois scrambled around the fire to the picnic tables. Harold snapped off two more shots. Jacob dumped a box of shells onto the table and reloaded. He looked up to see Clint running down his front steps with the SKS in his hand. Jacob cocked the shotgun and scanned the north end of the circle. "Harold, *look out*."

A figure emerged from the corner of Gwen and Penny's house. Jacob raised the Benelli, waited for the shot, and fired. The man faltered and fell to the ground as his shin folded in half. He hissed in pain. Harold sidestepped and finished him off.

Clint upended the empty picnic table. Francois joined him behind it, and they steadied the barrels of their guns on the edge of the bench. Six strangers came down the road, and another found their way in past the Miller's. Two more emerged from the near side of Harold's house. Jacob staggered his shots, making sure he fired while the others reloaded. A halo of blood and tissue soaked into the snow around the circle, and bodies littered the area.

Jacob finished loading and cocked the Benelli. "You see any more?"

Francois squinted into the darkness. "Not yet."

Harold cupped a hand to his mouth and shouted. "Clint, *on your six.*"

Clint turned to see a figure moving toward them from the south. "Jesus, Davie, what the hell are you doing?"

Davie stopped three meters away from his brother but did not speak. His bloodshot eyes flickered with the light of the fire. He twisted his upper body to turn around, but instead, dropped to his knees and forward onto his hands. He bucked and heaved, at first only bile, but soon a thick, black substance dripped from his lips. Francois recoiled and covered his mouth as it splashed on the ground.

Davie looked up to his brother. Streaks of crimson seeped from the corners of his eyes and ears. Steam rose from his skin.

"Oh my God, Davie…"

Harold shouted again. "*We've got incoming.*"

Francois surveyed the silhouettes moving along the road, then glanced to Davie. Two figures neared the circle, maneuvering around bodies on the ground.

"Son of a bitch." Francois raised his shotgun and took aim.

Davie's head snapped left and right. His eyes locked onto Francois through blood and steam. Clint froze in place. He watched Davie stand, take two steps, and launch his full weight into Francois. Francois screamed as he lost his balance and fell to the ground. A shot came from the north end of the circle. Then another. Davie slashed with his hands and bit at Francois' face. Clint hesitated, but jumped forward and drove the butt end of the SKS against Davie's temple. Davie collapsed on top of Francois.

"Get this fucking guy off me." Francois pushed and kicked Davie's unconscious body off to his side. His eyes were wide and bright in contrast to his blood-stained face. He scrambled to his feet, breath short and choppy, and stared at his hands and the mess on the front of his coat.

Tears welled in Clint's eyes, and his lower lip trembled. He looked to his brother, dropped the rifle, and rested both hands on top of his head.

Jacob ran up next to Francois. "Are you okay?"

Francois wiped at his face. "Do I look fucking okay?"

"Hold on." Jacob picked up a tea towel from the ground by the fire. Francois snatched it and patted down his face with both hands. He lowered the towel. "So?"

Jacob inspected Francois' face. "A couple scratches. It doesn't look too bad."

Francois fell quiet. His lips thinned, and his eyes darted back and forth.

Jacob spotted Mati in the kitchen window of his house. Gwen stood on her porch, wrapped up in her housecoat. She held out a questioning hand with her palm up. Jacob shook his head. Gwen frowned and went back inside.

Jacob stood next to where Davie laid prone on the ground and watched him breathe in short, shallow bursts. One hand had an intermittent twitch. The snow turned translucent around him. Jacob nudged him in the ribs with the toe of his boot. Davie's arm shifted, and he gave a low moan.

Clint stood and stared.

Jacob put a hand on his shoulder. "Clint." He did not move. "Clint, man, come on."

Clint blinked, and with a deep breath, turned his eyes to Jacob.

"Listen, I know this is hard, but I need you to go get some towels and bandages. I'll stay here and watch Davie. I promise nothing will happen."

Two shots echoed in the darkness.

Jacob spun around. "Where the hell did that come from?"

Francois pointed past Gwen and Penny's house. "Sounded like it came from over there."

"Shit. It'll have to wait." Jacob waved an arm in front of Clint and locked eyes. "Towels and bandages, okay?"

Clint looked to Davie. He spoke in a quiet voice. "Okay."

"Good. Go, quick."

Clint walked backward a few steps. "I…I'll get some rope too."

"Yeah, that's probably a good idea."

Clint turned and ran toward his house.

THIRTY-EIGHT

Alex crouched in the snow with his pistol sighted. He swept it back and forth, waiting for movement. Satisfied that the others had moved on, he holstered the gun and walked to the steaming form two meters away.

Slumped face down in the snow, a dark stain spread out around their head. Alex lifted one shoulder with his boot and turned the body on its side. The man's eyes rolled back to show only white and his mouth had twisted into a frozen grimace. Alex dragged him by his feet back the same way he had come. At what felt like a safe distance, he heaped snow over the corpse until it blended in with the scenery. Once the task was completed, he paused to scan the darkness. With the only sign of activity being the faint glow of the fire at the community, he followed his own tracks to his hiding spot in the grove of trees.

A line of paracord, strung between two trunks, supported a poly tarp over the packed snow walls. After one last look around, Alex knelt and backed into the entrance of his makeshift tent. He sat back on his heels, rested his hands on his knees, and was still.

THIRTY-NINE

A pair of ravens flew over the Miller's house and into the adjacent trees. They spoke to each other in muted, cackling tones. Jacob pondered if they understood the situation happening around them, or if they cared.

His attention drew back to the scene in front of him. Davie sat with his hands tied behind him, an unwelcome addition to the carnage littering the community. He snapped and snarled like a rabid animal, testing the strength of the rope around his ankles and torso. Dark mess dripped down his chin and onto his chest. Thin lines of blood ran from his eyes and nose. Any exposed skin steamed like he stepped into the cold from a sauna.

The group gathered in a semi-circle around the chair, with Davie backlit by the fire. Clint and Erica huddled in the middle with their arms wrapped around each other. Jacob, Gwen, and Harold stood to their right, Francois and Nicolas to their left.

Harold crossed his arms. "Well, Ginger, what the hell are we doing here?"

Jacob looked up. "I don't know."

"If it were up to me, and pretty boy over there wasn't so emotional, I would've finished this already."

Gwen gasped with her eyes wide. "*Harold.*"

"Let's be serious, these things are dangerous. He's dangerous. Tying him up like some one-act freak show makes it that much worse."

Francois scratched under his jaw. "We need to understand what's going on here, maybe Davie can help us with that."

Clint cried out. "That ain't Davie. *Not anymore.*"

Harold raised his rifle. "Then let's get this over with."

"*No.*" Jacob raised a hand. "Just stop. Everybody needs to calm down. We need to think about this for a minute."

Harold lowered his rifle and moved away. "Suit yourself. I'm going inside. Not going to freeze my ass off while you kids pussy-foot around."

Gwen frowned. "I'm afraid I'm with Harold on this one. You all talk amongst yourselves. I'll go get a pot of coffee started." She left the group and tended to her task around the opposite side of the fire.

Francois adjusted the zipper on his parka. "I'm going to head in, too."

"You sure you're all right?"

Francois turned to Jacob and gave a thumbs-up, but the look on his face offered a different impression. Lips drawn and eyes dark, he put his hands in his pockets and wandered off.

Erica wiped away the tears streaming down her cheek. "We should get inside and check on the kids."

Clint sighed, and his breath caught in his throat. "Yeah."

Walking home, they took each other's hand. Clint looked

back, only for a moment, then they followed the path to the porch and went inside their house.

Jacob looked around the circle. He focused on the Miller's house, then Davie. He held his watch close to his face and his ear, listening for the faint ticking of the mechanism.

"Nicolas, I need to go check on something. Can you stay here for a few minutes?"

"I...I suppose so." Nicolas drew in a cold breath and held it.

Jacob handed him the Benelli by the forestock. "Just hang tight, I won't be long."

Nicolas held the shotgun with both hands, but at an odd angle. He swallowed hard and glanced over his shoulder at Davie.

Walking past the wood pile, Jacob picked up the axe before carrying on to the Miller's front porch. He set the axe head on the ground and leaned the handle against the railing. At the door, he knocked hard three times and stepped back. While he waited, he stared at his boots. Not a single noise came from inside the house. Jacob descended the steps, grabbed the axe by the handle, and walked slow down the side of the Miller's house.

Tracks in the snow led in both directions from the back door. Jacob had no idea how fresh they were, so he scanned the trees as the wind gusted fine snow over top of him. He reached out for the doorknob with his head low. Jacob did not expect it to, but the knob turned, and the door pushed free from the frame.

Poking his head inside, he paused, then backed in through the door and eased it shut. Nothing seemed out of the ordinary, except for the smell. The air hung thick and fetid.

Jacob held a hand over his mouth and inched from the cramped mud room into a hall.

He tried the first door but found it locked. At the next, he found the bathroom, with the shower curtain drawn tight across the tub. Jacob lifted the axe to shoulder height and stepped into the room. He reached out, but hesitated. Inhaling deep through his nose, he swiped the curtain open and jumped back. The tub was clean and empty. Jacob backed out of the bathroom and went on to the next room. Another locked door greeted him. He balled his free hand into a fist and moved past it.

The house opened to a dated kitchen on the left. The counters were clear, save for a drinking glass half-filled with water. A round oak table, with an elaborate lace doily on top, occupied the small dining area. Arranged around the table, four matching chairs with plush fabric cushions.

Jacob worked his way to the living room. Along the wall, a sofa was piled high with blankets, dark velvet pillows flanking each end. A flat screen TV rested on a solid oak stand across from it. An upholstered rocking chair at the front bay window seemed to be in the perfect position for keeping a close eye on the neighborhood.

The floor creaked behind him. As Jacob turned to look, shocking pain exploded at the back of his head. He stumbled forward and raised his arms.

"What the hell do you think you're doing?" George stood in front of him with an aluminum baseball bat in his hands, his eyes frantic.

"Mr. Miller, I can explain."

Jacob flinched as the bat swung down again, but he blocked it with his forearms.

"I'll teach you to trespass." George swung again and again, catching Jacob on his shoulder and the side of his face.

Jacob moved around and retreated until he backed up against the kitchen table. George moved in for another attack. Jacob blocked with his left and raised the axe with his right. He swung the axe blind. It deflected up after making contact. George cried out and dropped the bat. Jacob blinked through the pain, gripped the axe handle with both hands, and lunged out with the aft end. It landed with a dull thud. Jacob pinched his eyes tight as blood sprayed his face. George let out a thin breath and collapsed to the floor.

Jacob sat in the corner of the Miller's living room, trying to calm his breath. Ice crystals clicked against the aluminum eaves outside. When the wind gusted against the thin windowpanes, they rattled and shook. Otherwise, the house held an eerie silence. Perspiration dripped into his eyes. He moved to wipe it away, but at the last second held fast.

George laid on his back at the transition from the dining room to the living room and faced the ceiling with unblinking eyes. A dark pool stained the floor under his head.

Jacob brought the axe close to his side. He had not meant to hit George as hard as he did. It was a reaction, one he wished he could take back. He tightened his grip on the axe handle and waited for any sign of movement. When none came, Jacob used it as a crutch to push himself upright. Weak on his feet, he held one arm out for balance and looked around the room.

He used a colorful patchwork blanket from the arm of the couch to cover George. Standing over the body, he made an attempt to apologize or pray in his own way. After starting and stopping a few times, he left to check the rest of the house.

Jacob paused in front of the locked door closest to the living room and leaned the axe next to it. He braced himself against the opposite wall and set the heel of his boot under the doorknob. It required little effort for the wood frame to give. With a snap, the door flew open. He shook his hands out beside him and pushed out a long exhale.

Stacks of cardboard boxes lined one wall, with a set of folding TV trays leaning on them. An old office chair rested in the middle of the room. In the back corner, a tall metal coat rack had been heaped with reusable grocery bags and a pink umbrella.

Jacob frowned and stepped back out of the room. He looked to the front of the house, then down the hall toward the back door. He entered the room and looked along the inside wall to a bank of sliding closet doors. The room felt claustrophobic. Jacob tilted an ear. A familiar hum carried through the air, one that had been missing for the last few days.

Standing in front of the middle set of closet doors, he shoved them aside. Rough plywood shelving filled the space. Cans of food, toilet paper, and cleaning supplies packed the left side. On the right, heaps of military-looking metal boxes, and devices covered in dials and blinking lights. A makeshift desktop with organized piles of paper, pens, and bits of electronics made up the middle. Tucked in the corner, a bundle of zip tied wires rose up through the ceiling. A line of conduit teed off to a power box, and a bank of batteries nestled on the floor. Jacob scratched at his temple, scanning his memory for any indication of solar panels on the roof or garage. He realized that if he had not, George intended it that way. Jacob slid the doors closed and continued his sweep of the house.

Past the bathroom, at the end of the hall, he faced the rear entrance. Along the right side sat a washing machine, dryer, and a shelf with cleaning supplies. Taking a step back, Jacob paused in front of the second locked door. His eyes scanned all around him and settled on the doorknob, keyed like the first. He sighed and looked down the hall. "Dumbass."

Jacob returned to kneel beside George's body. He pulled the blanket away to reveal dull skin and eyes beginning to cloud. He patted the pockets of George's jacket, pausing at the chime of metal on metal. He reached in and extracted a ring of keys. Spread out in his hand, he counted seven in all. One for the Miller's Buick and two smaller for a lock or storage box. The rest were standard house keys, each with a colored dot on the face. George's meticulous nature spread to more than the lawn.

The third key Jacob tried, one with a purple dot on it, opened the Miller's bedroom door. He covered his nose and mouth with his left hand as it swung wide, and blinked away the stinging in his eyes. The room stood dark. Instinctively, Jacob reached out for the light switch inside the door. Three ornate lightshades came to life, and the blades of a ceiling fan began a slow rotation.

At first glance, the room appeared much like the rest of the house, simple furnishings and tidy. The scattering of wood frames on the dresser and wall held faded pictures of their family with bright teeth and wide smiles. Jacob pulled his shoulders forward and held his arm close, uncomfortable in a space so personal to someone intent on hiding everything about their life.

Darina's arms dangled from the posts of the headboard. Red stained rope cut through to bone at her wrists. The taught lines secured to the end of the bed frame wrapped around her ankles. By the looks of things, the footboard did not hold up as well as George hoped. It hung broken on one side. Blood saturated Darina's blouse and the sheets surrounding her. Spray extended to the wall behind her head and onto the floor. Her lips pulled back from her crooked jaw to show most of her teeth missing. Dried blood flaked on her cheeks and ears. Hazy, sunken eyes froze in a distant stare. Jacob worked backward, creating a timeline of the previous hours and days.

Jacob turned the lights off, stepped out of the room, and pulled the door shut. He turned the key to set the lock, then walked through the mud room and out the back door.

Nicolas jumped when Mati launched from her chair and ran past the fire. Jacob shuffled out from between the Miller's and the vacant house. Battered and swollen, he nearly lost his footing as he returned to the circle. Mati stopped beside him. He saw her expression and held out his hand. "It's okay. I'm okay."

"What happened?"

"George surprised me. I…he's dead."

Mati crossed her arms. "I thought I heard someone shout, but I wasn't sure. Was he…?"

"No. He wasn't sick. At least, I don't think so."

Nicolas joined Mati and Jacob. "What about his wife?"

"That's a different story." Jacob scanned the tables, then shuffled forward and grabbed a folded dish towel. He took it to the fire, dipped it in a pot of steaming water, and dabbed at his face. "Listen, I need to talk to everyone. There's a lot in there that they need to know about."

"Okay, I'll go get them." Nicolas strode away.

"Wait." Jacob turned to the north side of the fire. "What's going on with Davie?"

Nicolas paused. "When the sun came up, he went to sleep."

"That's it?"

"Yes."

Jacob eyed Davie slumped in his chair. "Okay. Thanks, Nicolas."

Nicolas nodded and ran off toward Francois and Rosana's house.

Jacob wiped his face again with the clean side, then threw the towel into the fire. Mati came up next to him. "You sure you're okay?"

"I don't know, I hope so. Is there water somewhere?"

"Yeah, hold on." Mati grabbed a bottle of water from the nearest picnic table and held it out for him.

"Thanks." He twisted off the cap and gulped it down. "Where's Gwen?"

"She went in to go to the bathroom."

"Okay." Jacob looked around the circle. "Looks like you guys have been busy."

Toward the entrance of the community, bodies from the night before laid side by side, covered in bed sheets. Rocks and packed snow held the corners in place. Fresh snow had been brought in to cover the blood. Shovel imprints marked the compressed top layer.

"That was Nicolas. He said he didn't want them sitting there like that. Any IDs he found are on the table."

Gwen and Deborah appeared behind them.

"Oh, my word, Jacob. What happened?"

"George happened. Don't worry, I'll explain when everyone gets here."

Francois trailed down the path from his house. Dark circles lined his empty eyes. Hands deep in his pants pockets, he frowned and motioned toward Jacob. "Are you all right?"

"Yeah, should be."

"Should be?"

Jacob lowered his eyes and nodded.

Silent, Francois turned away.

Nicolas walked in from behind him. "Clint will be out soon, he's getting dressed."

Penny escorted Harold to the fire and guided him to a seat. Her eyebrows pinched together as she eyed Jacob, but she said nothing. The group turned at the sound of a door slamming. Clint sprinted down his porch steps. He concentrated on Davie as he neared. "Okay, I'm here. What the hell is goin' on?" Clint looked to Jacob. "Jesus, man, are you okay?"

"I'm fine."

"What happened?"

"I had a bad feeling, so I snuck into the Miller's place. George surprised me, but that's not the biggest problem. I found Darina. She was sick."

Clint crossed his arms. "Was?"

"She's gone now."

All color drained from Francois' face. He watched Davie from the corner of his eye. "I need to see this."

"Are you sure?"

Francois nodded.

Jacob pulled the ring of keys from his pocket and tossed them to Francois. "The room at the end of the hall is their bedroom. Purple key."

Francois raised an eyebrow and paused. "You kept it locked?"

Jacob shrugged. "I'm not sure why. It seemed like the right thing to do at the time."

"I'll be back." On his way past, Francois lifted a shotgun from the picnic table. At the Miller's front door, he fussed with the keys until he found the right one. The door clicked shut behind him.

Jacob turned his attention to the group. "Listen, that's not all. George has a room in there that's full of electronics. Everything is working. They've still got power."

Clint scowled. "What? You're kidding me, right?"

"I'm not. There has to be something we can use to communicate with the outside world, but I have no idea what half of it is."

Nicolas raised a hand. "Let me have a look, I might be able to figure it out."

"Okay, good. I'll go with you. I forgot the axe."

The Miller's front door opened. Francois stepped out to the porch. The grim look on his face told the group everything they needed to know. He passed by and lobbed the keys to Jacob. "I'm not feeling too good. Need to lay down for a bit."

Francois pulled the hood of his jacket over his face and headed home.

Clint watched Francois leave, then turned to Jacob. "Must be pretty bad if it's turned that boy's stomach."

"Yeah, it's not good."

"So, what's the plan?"

"Well, besides the electronics, George was stockpiling supplies."

"Like what?"

"Things we can use, it's like a convenience store in there. I'm pretty sure I saw survival gear too. Full on prepper type shit."

"I always thought people like that were crazy." Clint eyed the pile of bodies across the way. "Not so much anymore."

Gwen put her hand at Deborah's back. "Deb and I can help sort everything out if you like."

"That would be great. I'd like to take care of George first, though."

Nicolas cleared his throat. "I can give you a hand with that as well."

Jacob gave a wary smile. "Thank you. Let me just—"

His words fell flat against the thud of a gunshot. Clint was already running when the second shot rang out. He vaulted the steps of Francois' porch and shook the locked door. He took a step back and rammed his full weight into it. The door snapped open and Clint passed through the open frame.

FORTY

Francois eased the door closed behind him and set the lock. Rosana would be upset with boot prints on the floor, but he did not take them off. She worked hard to keep the house clean and presentable. The concern barely registered as Francois' mind raced on. He could not remember being as scared as he felt then. The world ceased to make any sort of sense.

He pushed the bedroom door open but stopped halfway when the hinges complained. Muted sunlight washed over the room. Rosana laid bundled up on the right side of the bed with half of her face showing. Francois perched on the end, careful not to disturb her. He watched the slow rise and fall of the comforter. A shaky smile came to him, and tears rolled down his cheeks. He spoke in hushed tones to his sleeping wife.

"I don't know that I understood what love meant before I met you. My purpose in this life has been to keep you happy and safe." He wiped his clammy forehead with the back of his hand. "Now, I don't know if that is possible." He raised the tips of his fingers from his lips to the air toward Rosana. "I will always love you. Toujours, mon amour."

Francois pulled the strap of the Benelli from his shoulder. He blinked away fresh tears and leveled the barrel at Rosana's slumbering form. "I'm so sorry."

The flash left him disoriented. Ringing in his ears stole all other sound. Facing away from Rosana, he planted the butt plate of the rifle between his feet. He craned his neck out and rested the end of the barrel in the crook above his Adam's apple. The heat from the barrel made him flinch at first, but he settled and adjusted the angle of the gun. With a shaky exhale, Francois closed his eyes and pushed his right index finger down on the trigger.

FORTY-ONE

It seemed an eternity before Clint walked out through Francois' front door. His shoulders slumped, and silent tears tracked down his face. He met the group with red eyes and shook his head.

Erica stood at the bottom of the porch steps, chewing the nails on one hand as the other arm rested across her torso. Clint faltered coming down Francois' steps, so he put a hand on the railing to steady himself. He walked straight to Erica. She put an arm around his shoulder and led him home.

Tears formed in the corners of Deborah's eyes. She clenched her jaw and set off toward Gwen's house as fast as her legs would carry her.

Jacob set the heel of his hand against his temple. "What the hell is happening?"

Deborah came out of the house with two plastic bags in her hand. Penny followed her. "Deb, please…"

Gwen turned as Deborah passed by. "Deb? What are you doing?"

"I'm going home."

"What are you talking about? You can't go off by yourself."

"Course I can. I'm a grown woman last time I checked."

"But you'll be safer here."

She stopped and looked right at Gwen. "Safe?" She swept her arm across the community. "You call this safe? If this is what we have to look forward to, then I'm going to face it on my own terms and in my own home." Her lips trembled. She looked to each person, daring them to disagree. Gwen averted her eyes and put a hand over her mouth. Deborah pulled her jacket closed and walked on. At the trees laid across the road, she lost her footing. She fell to her knees and dropped her bags.

Penny called out. "*Gwen.*"

Gwen wiped tears from her eyes and looked up. She set her jaw and marched out of the circle to where Deborah sat in the snow. She held out her hand. "Get off your ass, you dumb old broad. You're setting a bad example."

Deborah hung her head, and her body shook as she cried. "I can't."

"You sure as hell can. You've been through too much to give up now."

Deborah coughed and drew in a rattled breath as she grabbed Gwen's hand.

"That's better. Come on." Gwen helped Deborah to her feet and picked up her bags. She looped her hand through the crook of Deborah's arm and brought her back toward the fire. Deborah fumbled in her pocket for her inhaler and took a puff. They kept to the perimeter of the circle as they walked the cleared path to Gwen's front door. Deborah looked up to the group. Gwen did not.

Jacob sighed and lowered his head. "Damnit."

Nicolas turned from Francois' house to Clint's, then to Jacob. "What do we do?"

Jacob's chin trembled. "I don't know." He ran a hand through his hair and shook his arms out.

Nicolas pushed his glasses up his nose. "Do you…I mean, do you still want to sort out the situation with George and Darina?"

Wiping at his eyes, Jacob looked to Francois and Rosana's half-open front door. "Yeah, I just need a minute. I'll meet you there?"

Nicolas nodded. "Of course. Take your time."

Jacob focused on the ground and walked toward Francois and Rosana's front door.

After dragging George through the threshold of his bedroom, Jacob locked the door, removed the key from the ring, and slipped it underneath. He stopped at the bathroom for a dose of hand sanitizer, then proceeded down the hall. Still rubbing his hands together, he leaned through the doorway to George's secret room. Nicolas bent over the small desk, fiddling with knobs and flipping levers.

"How are things going in here?"

Nicolas settled back into the desk chair. "To tell the truth, I'm not sure. He's got quite the collection. I found a scanner. It's been cycling for twenty minutes, but I'm only finding static. Some of the other equipment is confusing. It's pretty old. I think he's even got a telegraph back on the shelf."

Jacob browsed the collection of gadgets. "Weird."

"It's not all bad." Nicolas picked up a black and silver box resembling a large walkie talkie. "This is a HAM radio. I've only been listening so far, but I've picked up some local conversations."

"Really? What are they saying?"

Nicolas shot a look at Jacob over the frame of his glasses. "It's not good, especially in the more populated areas."

Jacob frowned. "Yeah, that's sort of what we thought." He scratched at one earlobe. "Hey, I know the chances are slim, but can you try sending a message out?"

"Let me see what I can do."

"Thanks, Nicolas. I'll start moving some of the food out of here, then I'm going to go get cleaned up, and maybe lay down for a bit. Come find me if anything comes up, okay?"

"Don't worry, I will."

———

Jacob rolled over in bed. He reached for his watch and held it in front of his face. "Shit." The hand showed a quarter past five. Jacob flipped the sheets to the side, slipped on his boots, and ran out the door.

The shadows were long as Jacob made his way to the circle. Clouds, tinted a dirty orange with the haze of the world burning around them, scattered across the sky. Gwen and Mati tidied up the picnic tables. Mati noticed him approaching, then watched Gwen from the corner of her eye.

"Hey, Gwen. Sorry, I didn't mean to sleep that long."

"It's okay, dear. You obviously needed it." She wiped her hands on a towel and flipped it over her shoulder. "I assume you were the one who left everything out front of my place?"

"Yeah, I wasn't sure what else to do with it."

"I took care of it, don't worry."

Jacob smiled and lowered his eyes. "Thank you."

Gwen carried a stack of dishes home, and Jacob settled in one of the chairs by the fire. Sam nudged his hand with her muzzle. Mati sat down in the chair next to them. "Hey."

Jacob scratched behind Sam's ear. "Hey."

When he looked up, Mati held her focus on him and gave a sad smile. "You okay?"

Jacob lifted his eyes to the horizon and squinted against the burning light. "Maybe. Not sure."

Mati twisted a loose string around her finger. "You keeping watch tonight?"

"Don't think I have much of a choice."

"Is it okay if we join you?"

"You think that's a good idea?"

"Sure. Why not?"

"I can come up with a bunch of reasons."

Mati chewed on her lip and smiled. "Maybe you need some backup?"

Jacob let loose a dry laugh. "Sure. Okay."

"Good, it's settled." Mati leaned back in her chair and pulled a tattered paperback from her coat pocket.

"What are you reading?"

"I don't know. Found it on the shelf."

"Is it any good?"

"Not really."

"Then why are you reading it?"

"What else is there to do?"

Jacob shrugged. "Fair enough."

Gwen appeared behind them and held a bottle of water in front of Jacob. "I forgot to mention, there's a plate wrapped up by the fire when you're ready."

Jacob took the bottle. "Thank you."

Gwen squeezed Jacob's shoulder and turned to walk home. She stopped two steps in and looked back with a frown.

Erica shuffled toward the circle in baggy sweats and untied runners. She held a plastic shopping bag in one hand and a can of beer in the other. Her eyes focused on the packed snow at the trio's feet. "Hi."

"How is everything going, dear?"

Erica shrugged. "Just needed to get out of the house, you know?"

Gwen crossed her arms. "How's Clint?"

Erica looked across the fire to Davie hunched over in the chair. "Not good. Said he can't do it anymore."

Jacob tilted his head to better focus on her eyes. "What do you mean?"

"He asked me to bring you this." Erica set the bag down on the table and tucked her hand under the opposite arm. "It's the rest of the ammo."

She looked back to the house, then turned to face the group. "Listen, I just wanted to say thank you, for everything you guys have done. It means a lot that you'd look out for us like that." Her lip quivered, and tears built in her eyes.

Gwen softened her stance. "If we can't look out for each other, then what do we have?"

Erica wiped her face with her sleeve. Her lips formed a sad, weak smile. "Okay, I'd better head in." She began the slow trudge back home.

"Jacob?"

Jacob spun around. "For the love of..." He let out a long exhale. "You scared the shit out of me."

Nicolas pulled at his right ear. "Sorry."

"You've been at the Miller's this whole time?"

"I have. I was really hoping to make contact, but nothing worked. I was frustrated, so I kept trying."

"No luck, then?"

Nicolas shook his head. "I tried everything. On the radios, I could hear conversations, but for some reason they could not hear me. I charged my phone, but there's still no signal."

"Okay, we can try again tomorrow, I guess."

Gwen motioned to the fire. "Would you like some dinner, dear? I can heat up some leftovers."

"No, thank you. I should go see Malena."

Gwen nodded.

Nicolas gave an embarrassed smile and waved them farewell.

"All right, I need to head in. Be back shortly."

"Okay. Thanks, Gwen."

Jacob took a long drink and capped the bottle of water. He sank back in the chair and scratched at his thigh.

Mati leaned forward in her seat. "So…"

"So, what?"

Mati pushed her hand out of her sleeve and rubbed the side of her nose. "What now?"

Jacob shrugged. "I don't know." His eyes skimmed around the circle, but he avoided the boards nailed over Francois and Rosana's front door. "I think tomorrow we need to bulk up the barricades." He motioned off to their right. "We should also check the abandoned house. Might have left something behind we could use."

"You think it will do any good?"

"No guarantees, but we have to try."

Mati's eyebrows drew together. She raised her head to watch the night sky. "What do you think you'll do, you know, when this is all over?"

"You mean, if we make it out alive?"

"Well, yeah."

"I don't know. I guess it depends on what the world looks like. Might find a nice Canadian girl, settle down, and repopulate the world." Jacob attempted a smile. "You know, the usual."

Mati lowered her head and grinned. "Sounds like fun."

"Hey, it's a big job, but somebody has to do it." Jacob stretched his arms over his head. "What about you? Have your plans changed?"

"I don't know. Not really."

"What does that mean?"

"It means I haven't decided yet. I'll still give school another shot. Need to figure out where, though."

"That's great. Really."

"Yeah. I hope the scholarships will still be there."

Jacob nodded. "Me too."

They watched the fire and listened to the pops and cracks of the glowing coals. Mati pulled the collar of her sweater up over her chin. "Do you think people will be different after this?"

"One way or another, they will be. How they'll be different is what I'm not sure of."

Mati pulled her knees up and wrapped her arms around them. "I mean, do you think people will be nicer? Like, will we treat each other better?"

"I hate to say it, but I don't think so. Not on any grand scale, anyway."

"Really?"

"Well, there are good people out there. If this whole mess has shown me anything, it's that people can come together when we have a common goal. Once the memory fades, things will go back to the way they were. Society puts up this façade that we're tolerant and accepting, that we want to take care of each other. If you really pay attention, underneath, it's always me against you. Us against them. Closed minds and closed hearts. We buy into stories that keep us afraid and separated. At least on a basic level, we're far more alike than we are different. The sooner everybody figures it out, the better off we'll be."

"Very philosophical of you."

Jacob shrugged. "I'm not saying I've had it bad, but with everything that's happened in the last few months, it's given me a lot to think about, you know?"

"So, you don't think there's anything to look forward to?"

"I'm sure there will be. Maybe I just focus on the bad stuff, or I can't let it slide as easily as other people do." Jacob twisted the water bottle in his hands. "I mean, really, what right do I even have to be complaining? I think about the things you've been through, and the things you've seen. I can't even imagine."

Mati shrugged and rested her chin on her knees.

Looking to the west, Jacob sighed. "The sun's almost down. Guess we'd better get ready."

He peeled himself from the chair and went to the picnic table. The shopping bag handles rustled in the soft breeze. Jacob pulled them open. At the bottom sat two small boxes, each with the top flaps pulled back. He counted three shells in one and two in the other. Jacob looked up the road and exhaled out of his nose, counting under his breath. He patted the empty pockets of his jacket. "Shit."

Mati turned. "What?"

"Nothing." Jacob picked up the remaining loose shells and slipped them into his pocket.

———

Shadows crept in from the horizon and settled over the community. Davie made small movements, pulling at his restraints and moaning.

Jacob stood and tucked the shotgun in the crook of his arm. He watched Davie through the sparks and heat of the fire. A door opened and closed to his left, but he kept his focus. Slow, crunching footsteps moved closer along the snow-covered path.

"Hello, dear."

"Hey, Gwen."

Harold fell in beside Jacob. "I wouldn't worry too much. He's not going anywhere."

Jacob kicked at the ground. "I know." He leaned the shotgun against the arm of his chair and sat down. "What are you guys doing out here, anyway?"

Gwen sat beside him with a tote bag on her lap. "Wouldn't want to miss out on the fun, now would we?"

She pulled a stack of plastic cups from the tote and set them in the mesh holder on the arm of her chair. Next, she placed a half empty bottle of gin between her feet and her .357 on her lap. Jacob stared at the pistol. Gwen separated a cup and leaned down for the gin. "Who wants a drink?"

Harold rested his elbows on the arms of his chair. "You know it."

Jacob shrugged. "Sure, why not."

Gwen poured and handed off the cups. She turned to Mati. "How about you, dear?"

Mati tucked her arms inside her sweater and gave a thin smile. "Thanks, but I'm good."

"All right then, more for the rest of us." Gwen poured another glass almost full and put the bottle between her feet.

Jacob took a sip from his cup and sank back as the warmth spread through his body. Harold sat upright in his chair. "So, think we're in for a busy night?"

"I sure hope not."

Harold squinted, moving his eyes between Jacob and the gun propped up next to him. "What's the ammo situation?"

Jacob stared at the ground. "Not what I would like it to be."

Harold scowled and looked to the fire. "I've only got a few left myself. We've got Gwen's pistol. Think we should get the other one back from the Frenchman? Or from Clint?"

"I don't think Clint will give his up. I tried to go in and grab the other shotgun before I boarded up the house. I…I just couldn't"

"It's okay, son. Probably won't make much difference anyway." Harold picked up his cup of gin, lifted it to his lips, and tilted it back. Lowering the cup, he motioned to the other side of the fire. "What're we doing about that?"

Davie slumped forward. Warmth from his breath and his skin mixed in the air and drifted away.

Jacob sighed. "Honestly? I don't know."

"We're going to just let him sit there, then?"

"What other choice do we have?"

"We have the same choice we've been exercising on every other person who comes around with his particular dilemma. I don't understand why it should be any different."

"I don't know. It's Davie. Maybe he deserves something better."

"Something better? Jesus H. Christ, if you want something better, then put him out of his misery. There's only one ending here. The way I see it, it's either by our hand, or we let him suffer. I keep thinking that if it was a dog tied up over there, he would have been put down long ago."

Gwen took a sip from her glass and settled her eyes on the fire. "That's no dog, Harold, that's a human being."

"Listen woman, when I was in the war, there was always a struggle. You're taking the life of another human being because of where they come from, or what their government says that you don't agree with." Harold pointed a shaking hand at Davie. "That right there isn't human anymore. The choice shouldn't be so hard."

Gwen turned away.

"Give the word, Ginger. Nothing will be held against you."

Jacob pursed his lips. "I don't know if I can."

Faint rhythms of movement drummed in the dark, and a familiar scent drifted in on the breeze.

Jacob stood. "Shit."

Gwen slid to the edge of the chair and set her hand on her pistol.

Jacob grabbed the shotgun by the forestock and moved around the fire to stand beside Davie. When his eyes adjusted to the lack of light, he scrambled back. A group of shadows moved up the worn path in the road. Jacob stepped away from the fire and glanced to the east. More figures advanced between the abandoned house and the Miller's.

Sam snarled and darted to the woman in the lead. Her braided blonde hair wove tight around her steaming head, and one punctured eye dangled above a shredded cheek. Sam spread her paws wide and barked an urgent warning. The woman moved to go around, but Sam intercepted. The woman kicked at Sam's head, but she shied away.

Mati sprinted past the wood pile and lifted the handle of the axe. She stopped in front of Sam and swung out. The head of the axe cracked bone and planted deep into the woman's clavicle. Mati jerked the axe free as the woman stumbled. She wrapped her fingers around Sam's collar and retreated. When a safe enough distance away, a shot rang out, and the woman fell. Mati saw Harold with his rifle aimed to the distance behind her. She ducked low and slunk to the back of the circle.

Gwen braced herself and fired her magnum. The bullet tore through the throat of a man wearing a denim vest over a white long-sleeved shirt. He grabbed at his neck and fell forward to the ground. Dark, greasy locks of hair and blood splayed out in the snow.

Jacob raised the shotgun and sighted. He took in a deep breath and held it. His heart hammered in his chest as he squeezed the trigger, again, and again. When he knelt to reload, Harold fired over him along the road. Gwen shot once at a young girl emerging from the shadows by the Miller's house, then joined Harold.

Jacob shouldered the shotgun and fired until it ran empty. He reloaded and emptied it again. The air fell silent, like someone had pressed the mute button. Jacob looked behind him to Gwen and Harold, then turned to the barricade. Crooked arms, broken skulls, and gore littered the felled trees like macabre decoration.

Jacob focused up the road. He swore under his breath and ran to the back side of the fire.

Gwen rested a hand on his arm. "Jacob, what's wrong?"

"I'm out." Jacob fought to catch his breath. "And we've got more incoming."

Gwen's lips tightened, and she looked to Harold. He frowned and shook his head.

Gwen faced the road and sighed. "All right, then."

A woman with one good eye, wearing blood-stained overalls, climbed over the bodies and stacked trees at the barricade. A man, in only his underwear, waded into the deeper snow to the left.

The night sky cracked, and a pulse of air brushed by Jacob's ear. The man collapsed, the spray of blood from his temple illuminated by the firelight. Jacob dropped to his knees. Another shot, and the woman fell back and laid still in the snow.

Jacob spun, hunting in the darkness for movement. Mati and Gwen huddled together on the ground. Harold stood, but braced one hand on the back of the nearest chair for support.

"What the hell" A flash lit up Jacob's peripheral, and another shot sounded out. The silhouette of a body fell from the shadows beside the abandoned house.

Jacob dropped the gun on the ground and knelt with his hands over his head. Closing his eyes, he let out a slow, trembling breath.

He only opened his eyes when Mati and Sam shimmied up beside him. Mati whispered by his ear. "Do you hear that?"

Jacob lifted his chin. "Hear what?"

"Does that sound like a truck to you?"

Sam barked an alert. She broke loose from Mati's grasp, sprinted off toward Jacob's house, and disappeared around the porch.

Mati yelled after her. "Sam, *get back here.*"

Her barking changed, it became high pitched and insistent. Sam raced to the fire and hid behind Mati.

Jacob stood and stepped away to focus on the dark space

along the side of his house. He heard rustling movement but saw nothing.

Mati's voice wavered. "Jacob, what's going on?"

"I don't know. Maybe they're going around." Jacob's face grew pale. He looked to Gwen and Harold, then swallowed hard. "I'm…I'm just going to check it out."

"Jacob, no."

Jacob held his hand down. "It's okay. I won't get too close."

He walked the path to his house, his steps slow and precise. At the porch, he stopped to listen, fighting the urge to look back to the fire for reassurance.

His heart hammered at his chest, and his breath came short and sharp. Rounding the porch, he continued into the darkness. Footprints littered the ground at the back of the house. Movement sounded light in the air. Small glints of reflected light flashed in the distant snow.

Jacob looked over his shoulder toward the circle. Harold stood near the top with his rifle ready but pointed low. Gwen gripped her gun in her right hand and waved Jacob back with her left.

Jacob faced the darkness once again, but the light from the fire reversed what night vision he had gained. He spun on his heel and ran back to the group.

Everyone held still, waiting, but they did not have to wait long. At first, the crackle of a radio echoed, then an unseen voice erupted from the dark. "This is Sergeant Bernard Harmon with the thirty-second Canadian Brigade Group. Lower your weapons, *now*."

Harold set his rifle against the arm of his chair and sat down. "About damn time."

From the trees to the east came shouting. A gun discharged, then another.

Jacob held his breath as he watched two figures emerge from around his house. One marched forward with their face lowered to the scope of a serious looking weapon. The second trailed a step or two behind, with a large pack strapped across their back. A respirator covered the bottom half of their face.

Decorated head to toe in mottled green camouflage and brown leather straps, the pair halted at the top of the path to the circle. A voice called out, steady but tired. "Have any of you come into direct contact with the infected?"

Jacob shook his head, not wanting to look in Mati's direction. "We're okay."

The soldier in the lead scanned the group over top of his rifle's scope. His eye trailed to Gwen's lap, and his grip tightened.

"If you think I'm dropping it in the snow, you're out of your mind."

"On the ground. I won't ask again"

Gwen scowled, then set her pistol on the tote bag beside her chair.

The soldier focused across the fire to Davie. "What's up with him?"

"He's…sick."

The soldier turned his head to the side but kept his eyes forward. He spoke under his breath to his partner with the heavy pack, then to the group. "Why is he tied up?"

"He's one of us."

The soldier with the rifle crept around the fire, stopping a few paces from Davie and dropped to one knee. He pulled a flashlight from a pocket on his vest and clicked the button.

Davie howled when the light passed over his face, spitting blood as he thrashed in his restraints. The soldier moved to Davie's left, raised the rifle to his temple, and squeezed the trigger. Jacob blinked his eyes as the muzzle flash repeated in his vision. Davie's head rolled to the side, and his body fell slack.

The soldier moved in the direction of the Miller's house, watching Jacob and the others as he went. He kicked one of the rocks holding a sheet over collected bodies and lifted a corner. "Is this all of them?"

"No, there's more behind the house over that way."

"Are the houses clear?"

"No."

"Which aren't?"

Jacob pointed to the Miller's, and to Francois and Rosana's.

"How many survivors?"

Jacob swallowed. "Oh. I...I haven't thought about it like that. There's the four of us, and, uh, nine others, I guess."

The soldier nodded and marched to the south. He met three others from the unit as they walked out of the shadows. One of the soldiers lowered his head to a radio attached to his vest. Jacob could not understand the message as garbled voices answered from the tiny speaker.

Gunfire cracked in the distance. The echoes made it hard to tell from where. The soldiers turned to each other again. The one with the radio motioned across the circle. The shortest of the group raised a thumb over their shoulder toward Clint's house and, after a quick conversation, jogged off toward the front door. The soldier with the radio moved past Francois' house. The remaining two came toward the group at the fire. The man in the lead stood tall, and his arms stayed wide at his sides as he walked. Harold gripped the arm of his chair and straightened his posture. "Evenin' Sergeant."

Sergeant Harmon looked sidelong at Harold and nodded. He raised his right hand and motioned to the soldier behind him. "This is Private Kanyuk." The soldier carrying the oversized pack stepped forward. "He's going to check you over quick before we head out."

Private Kanyuk proceeded to Harold and raised his right hand. Harold flinched as a pinpoint of red light dotted his forehead. "Don't worry, just logging your temperature."

The Private sidestepped to test Gwen, then Jacob.

Kanyuk knelt next to Mati. She pulled Sam to the opposite side of her chair and stared at the ground. The Private positioned the thermometer close to her forehead then lowered the screen. His gaze darted from the readout to Sergeant Harmon, then to Mati.

"Do we have a problem?"

Kanyuk watched Mati's eyes. "Little high. Not enough to be worried about." He slipped the thermometer into a pocket on his belt and fell in behind Sergeant Harmon. "We're good."

"Excellent." Sergeant Harmon set his hands on his hips and addressed the group. "You've got fifteen minutes to head home and pack a bag of essentials. Leave your weapons, we'll tag them and keep them safe. Everything will be waiting for you when you arrive."

Harold scowled. "Arrive where?"

"The emergency shelter in Brampton. We're getting you out of here."

FORTY-TWO

Early morning sunlight broke through cracks in the flat, gray clouds. Alex shaded his eyes as he trekked down the deep tire tracks leading to the community. Every few steps, he looked to the sky and listened for the rotation of metal blades. A combination of luck and skill allowed him to avoid the military scouts the night before. Still, being exposed felt like pushing his luck.

Charred skeletons of the resident's houses smoldered. Small fires still burned in spots. Alex traced footsteps around the tables and fire in the circle, like a hunter stalking prey. Trampled, dirty snow thawed into compact patches. Under the shelter of an overturned camp chair, the plastic handle of a bag crinkled in the breeze. He freed it from the snow and spread it open. Inside, he found a pile of identification cards, wallets, and cell phones.

He flipped through each one, palming any bills he found. At one piece of ID, he paused and ran a thumb over the picture. He stared as if looking into a mirror. Alex tucked the license, and anything with the same name on it, into the growing collection of paper money. From under his armored vest, he removed his own wallet and took out his license, credit and debit cards, and social security card. Dropping them in the bag, he kicked it back under the chair. With the money and identification secured inside, he slipped his wallet into his vest. He stepped away, and after a final look around the community, Callen Pearson walked north out of the circle and hiked into the wilderness.

FORTY-THREE

Jacob drew in a short breath and sat up with a start. His eyes darted to the door and the cot across from him. As his racing heart calmed, heat from raging fires and the smell of burning human flesh faded. Shadows cast by the harsh flood lights danced along the side of his tent. A row over, two people talked in hushed voices.

He swung his feet down next to the duffle bag on the ground. It contained all his earthly possessions. Having fifteen minutes to pack and leave the community did not present an issue for him, unlike the other residents.

Jacob picked up a water bottle from beside his cot and held it up to find it almost empty. Twisting off the cap, he set the opening to his lips and drained it. He wiped his mouth with his forearm and capped the bottle.

The first two nights in the Brampton camp proved to be chaotic. Kits handed out when they arrived, with toiletries and a few basic necessities, had not lasted as long as anticipated. Food and water had to be rationed. Families became separated between camps and personal property misplaced. A short supply of outhouses and handwash stations made it difficult to maintain hygiene.

With power and cellular networks restored, many of those issues sorted themselves out, and the extent of the storm truly came to light. News networks focused on fear and conjecture as they tend to, but the real stories found an audience direct from the source on social media. People broke into the quarantine zone and live streamed what they found, corroborating the first-hand accounts coming from the camps.

In Fort Erie, rumors circulated of a young boy who killed his father but spared his mother and sister. Touted as a beacon of hope, some said it showed that the infected could be helped, or that some amount of humanity remained. Overwhelming evidence to the contrary proved otherwise, and soon enough, the story became relegated to myth.

In Buffalo, a priest turned in the middle of his sermon. Members of the congregation managed to tie him up without getting hurt. They prayed over him for sixty hours straight until he bled out. Three people got sick from cleaning up. Days later, one killed her entire family in the middle of the night. The neighbors found her in the backyard with the carcass of the family dog on her lap.

Jacob moved to the door of the tent and eyed the cot on the opposite side. Confident his roommate was asleep, he slipped outside. With his hands in his pockets, he walked toward the collection of steel barrels used as impromptu fire pits. He snuck glances at dimly lit faces as he passed. Downcast shadows did little to flatter tired and sunken eyes, red from the smoke or the weight of their situation.

He went on until he arrived at an intersection of construction fencing that separated one tent city from another. In the farthest reach of the firelight, backed into a corner, he recognized dark hair under a threadbare hoodie. Jacob went along the fence and crouched down with his back to it. He wiped at his nose. "Can't sleep?"

The figure on the other side did not move. "No."

"Me either."

They sat in silence for a time, listening to the movements of the other survivors around them.

Mati adjusted her position and tucked her hair behind her ear. "Gwen says they took Harold to the hospital yesterday. He's not doing too good."

Jacob lowered his head and rubbed at his brow. "Shit." Looking up, he frowned. "How did she find out, anyway?"

Mati shrugged. "You know how Gwen is."

"Shouldn't surprise me, I guess. Are you holding up okay?"

"I guess so."

"It's been a little quieter since they started letting people out."

"Yeah, true."

"Did you have an appointment today?"

Mati held a hand over the bandage on her arm. "I did."

"How are you feeling?"

"It makes me tired, but I'm okay."

"Have they figured anything out yet?"

"Not that they tell me. With the amount of blood they're draining, you'd think there would be enough vaccine for everyone by now."

Jacob smiled, but it quickly faded. "You get ahold of your dad yet?"

"Sort of."

Jacob looked over his shoulder. "What does that mean?"

Mati shrugged. "He's coming to get me tomorrow."

"Oh. That's good."

She did not respond.

"What about Sam?"

"She's at a foster in Kingston. We're going to pick her up on the way." Mati wiped at her eyes and fell quiet.

"Hey, I finally got a message back from Evan. I told you about him, we were friends back when I lived in Toronto. He's coming to pick me up on Sunday." Jacob reached into his pocket and pulled out a folded piece of scrap paper. He pushed it through a hole in the fence. "It's his number. When you get settled, give me a shout."

Mati sniffed and focused on the ground for a moment, then raised her head and took the paper. "Thanks."

Jacob rested his forearms on his knees and wrapped his hands together. "We're going to be okay."

"You think so?"

"I'm not sure why, but I do."

"I trust you."

Jacob leaned his head against the fence. He searched the sky for familiar stars. High above, a jet crossed, then once again the night fell still. Behind him, Mati yawned.

Jacob leveled his head and stifled a yawn himself. "Well, I should probably head back."

"Yeah." Mati reached out for the wire fence to pull herself up, then bent down for the thin gray blanket on the ground.

Rising to his feet, Jacob turned to face her. Mati pulled her hands into her sleeves and folded the blanket against her body. She looked at Jacob through the wires. A sad smile pulled at her mouth.

Jacob's expression softened. "Be safe, okay?"

Mati nodded. "You too."

"Talk to you soon?"

Mati lowered her eyes and pulled the blanket tighter.

"Hey." Jacob rapped his knuckles on the fence. "Soon, right?"

Mati nodded. "I promise."

Jacob watched her walk away, then let out a long breath and turned to the yard. He scanned rows of tents and the few signs of life among them. At this time of night, most movement came from makeshift Christmas decorations rustling in the wind. People in the camp used whatever they could find to bring some sort of normalcy. Any trees within reach lost their branches to create rudimentary wreaths. Someone even wove an angel. Donated dollar-store decorations arrived the week before, but they did not last long when exposed to the weather.

The few stars visible in the glare of the yard lights washed out with the coming dawn. Jacob heard talk of snow. Clouds building to the north, and heaviness in the air, seemed to confirm the prediction. Even the idea of it brought tension to his chest.

Many things changed after the lights first went out, but as Jacob suspected, a great deal had not. People went back to their lives of distraction and distance in more ways than the physical sense. Still, some held out hope that society could learn. Hope, that a new day meant new opportunities. The problem was, each opportunity to be better also meant that the potential for a new type of storm existed, just across the horizon.

Thank you for reading!

Reviews are extremely important to indie authors. They help us hone our craft and find new readers. If you enjoyed this book, please consider sharing your thoughts on Amazon, Goodreads, or BookBub.

———

———

Also by Shane Kroetsch

This and That but Mostly the Other
Into the Storm (The Storm Series Book 1)
Chasing the Storm (The Storm Series Book 3)

ACKNOWLEDGMENTS

Life is pain. It's scary and uncertain. These truths have never been more apparent as we endure the chaos that a global emergency brings. I like to think I have a healthy imagination, but even I couldn't have guessed that when I started writing Surviving the Storm, almost five years ago, pathogen zombies wouldn't be the scariest thing we'd face in 2020.

It's easy to focus on the negative aspects of life. I do it too often. That's not what this is supposed to be about though. This space is to show appreciation for what got me here. So, for the moment at least, I'm going to focus on gratitude.

Thank you to the creatives who used the pandemic to practice and grow, and who pivoted to find ways to continue to do what they do in a time of such immense confusion. You've given us light in a time of darkness. This should never be ignored.

Thank you to those who support the creatives, whether in a financial sense, or by being their biggest fan when they need it most. Bringing our crazy ideas to the world is not possible, or worth it, without you.

Thank you to those who care for other people, whether as part of your profession, or because it's who you are. The world needs more love and understanding. We need as much kindness as we can get in a world that pushes us to be divided and afraid. You give me hope.

ABOUT THE AUTHOR

To date, Shane has released a collection of short fiction, a
zombie outbreak trilogy, and been featured in a growing
number of anthologies. In his spare time, he builds projects
out of old junk, paints watercolor blanket ghosts, and shakes
his butt while the vinyl spins.

The best way to keep up to date with his writing shenanigans,
including his current work in progress, and access exclusive
short stories is to subscribe at www.ShaneKroetsch.com.

9 781999 482060